To my dad, Richard William Tucker, for being my number one fan, and for not letting anything stop you from speaking or contributing to your community, and to my aunt and uncles—Kathy, Steve, and Neil. Thank you for sharing your memories and taking on the elders' mantle for us. This one is for the four of you.

This is an Arthur A. Levine book

Published by Levine Querido

www.levinequerido.com • info@levinequerido.com

Levine Querido is distributed by Chronicle Books, LLC

Library of Congress Control Number: 2021931871

ISBN: 978-1-64614-091-6

Printed and bound in China

Published September 2021

First Printing

MIGHTY INSIDE

by

Sundee T. Frazier

LEVINE QUERIDO

Montclair | Amsterdam | Hoboken

CHAPTER ONE

Melvin Robinson lay in the bottom of the bunk bed he'd been sharing with his older brother, Chuck, for almost all of his thirteen years. In one week, he thought, I'm dead meat.

He closed his eyes and imagined himself walking through Cleveland High's large wooden doors, saying the names of his friends and teachers in clear and confident tones, hearing himself say over and over, "Hi, I'm Melvin," to kids he met.

"Hi" was a good place for him to start because making the *H* sound was a lot like exhaling, and he could do that without getting tripped up. Usually.

Before lying down, Melvin had shut both bedroom doors. One led to the kitchen, the other to a short hall and the tiny bathroom all six in his family shared. He had closed the curtains over the two small, high windows to block the bright summer sun. He was trying to stay cool, and he was trying to stay calm.

He clicked on his reading lamp. His eyes roamed the space where he slept—his own private shelter. Over time, he had plastered the wall and the bottom of Chuck's bunk with maps Pops brought from train depots, and photos from *National Geographic*: Machu Picchu, the great pyramids of Egypt, Hopi caves in cliff walls. Images of

Roman aqueducts bridging chasms made him think of their own Monroe Street Bridge spanning the mighty Spokane River, which cascaded through downtown in a series of waterfalls.

Pops had told him the largest of these falls had been a gathering place for the area's first people, the Spokane Indians, before they were forced to live on a piece of "no-man's-land" by the government in 1881. Melvin's relatives had arrived in 1900 from North Carolina, and what they found in Spokane was apparently better than what they thought they could have in the South. They settled down, and now here he was, fifty-five years later, facing the biggest challenge of his life thus far: high school.

He stared at the Roman Colosseum on his wall. The stone stadium, with its three levels of arched openings, had once seated fifty thousand people and incorporated a retractable roof that had not been replicated in any of the great American stadiums, centuries later. Here, trained gladiators would take on wild animals and slay them or be slayed. Melvin was determined to see the Colosseum in person one day, but first, he had a battle of his own to win . . . at Cleveland High. *Go Tigers.*

He looked across the room to where his turtle, Tuck, sat in the small tank on his and Chuck's desk. Words flowed smooth as honey when he talked to his pet. All other times, he could never be sure. Some days he did okay. Other days, it was a nightmare.

Lately, every day was a nightmare.

He walked over to say hi. The turtle was submerged in the water around the little tropical island with the palm tree in the center. Only his snout showed. "I wish I could shrink myself and get in there with you, Tuck. If it were up to me, I'd do school right here in this room. Got my books, my magazines, my study space . . ." He gestured to his bunk, his place to hide. Like Tuck's shell, he thought. "*You*. What more do I need?"

He opened the desk drawer that he'd made very clear to the rest of his siblings, especially snoopy Maisy, they were never to pry around in, and pulled out the booklet that had come in the mail just the day before. "This right here, Tuck?" He flapped the booklet in the air. "This is the answer I've been waiting for!"

He went back to his bed, recalling the moment he had first seen the booklet advertised in *Popular Science*. It had appeared like a miracle, as if God and all His angels were shouting directly at him:

YOU CAN HAVE A HE-MAN VOICE!

His heart had beat a little faster. Eagerly, he had read on:

Send today for FREE booklet "Voice Power & Personal Power"
by Eugene Feuchtinger. Just send your name, address, and age.
Mailed in plain sealed envelope. No obligation. Write today!
PERFECT VOICE INSTITUTE, 325 W. Jackson Blvd., Chicago 6, Ill.

He could sound like a *he-man* instead of a broken record?

Shoot! Sign me up, he had thought.

With a perfect voice from the Perfect Voice Institute, he could speak up in class without fear. He could smooth-talk Millie Takazawa, the way he'd always dreamed.

He had rushed to his and Chuck's desk right then and there, written out the required information in his best handwriting, and sealed it in an envelope as the ad had instructed.

Now he held it in his hands: the key that would free his tongue from the shackles of the Stutter. "Mellifluous Melvin," they'd be calling him when they heard his smooth, baritone sounds, not only when he sang but when he spoke as well. Melvin stretched out on his bed, still gazing at the precious booklet with its promise of personal success and voice salvation, and opened to the first page. Testimonials with titles like "His Stutter Vanishes" and "Stammering Stopped" were so powerful, and filled him with such hope, that he wanted to read them again.

"Your instruction changed my voice from weak and pitiful to a free-flowing voice getting richer and stronger every day."

"I suffered from stammering for years. Four different courses in other methods brought no results. In six months after diligent practice in your wonderful, easily mastered lessons I received compliments on my smooth, clear voice. My inferiority complex has left me. Thanks to you, I am free from the stranglehold of stammering!"

And then this, direct from Mr. Feuchtinger himself: "A good voice! That's the magic key that opens the door to opportunity. What a glorious moment will be yours when your voice, without effort, soars and swells!"

Oh, yes! What a glorious moment, indeed. Or as they would say at Bethel A.M.E. Church, "Amen and amen!" May it be so.

He *needed* it to be so.

The bedroom door from the kitchen flew open and Chuck breezed in, along with the medicinal smell of Listerine. The boy used mouthwash more times a day than he used the toilet. Melvin shoved the Voice Power booklet under his backside and picked up the issue of *Popular Science* he'd been reading earlier.

"Hey, bro," Chuck said, pushing Melvin's magazine up so he could survey the cover, which read, "Be Prepared! Build Your Own Basement Bomb Shelter." He let out a dismissive *puh*.

Melvin winced at the smell. That Listerine stuff was way worse than any natural breath stink could ever be.

"Don't tell me you're falling for this whole 'The Commies Are Coming!' craze." He raised a single eyebrow at Melvin. "Look, I'll tell you what you really need to know to be prepared—for *high school*, which, unlike some atomic bomb dropping on us, is actually going to happen. Next week."

As if Melvin didn't know.

"In fact, I'll do you one better, little bro. I'll make you a list. So you can study it." Chuck sat at their desk and pulled out some paper and a pencil. "Studying is your thing, right?"

Chuck wasn't expecting an answer, of course. He had his back to Melvin and was busy writing. Chuck had spent the morning at Curtley's Cuts barbershop. The vanilla smell of Murray's Superior Hair Dressing Pomade—*much* better than Listerine—also wafted from his head. His hair was styled so tight it looked like you could bounce a quarter off it. The edges were pristine. Pops had invited Melvin to go as well, but he'd passed, claiming he didn't feel well, which was true. His stomach had been on edge for weeks.

They were quiet for the next several minutes, the only sound Chuck's scratching pencil. When he was done, he walked over and shoved a paper into the space between Melvin's face and the magazine.

Freshman Dos and Don'ts was written across the top in Chuck's cramped, tilted lettering.

"Follow my advice, and you won't end up hanging from a hook by your underwear in the girls' bathroom." Chuck jabbed at the column on the left. "Do these things, and you'll be good." He ran his finger solemnly down the column on the right. "These are the *Don'ts*. Do any of *these*, and you're a goner."

Melvin scanned his brother's list:

Dos

1. Carry your books on the side—two <u>max</u>, never a whole stack.

2. Be on time, never too early.

3. Walk into class like you're a king entering your domain.

4. Nod at upperclassmen. They like to be acknowledged.

5. Address teachers with their names.

6. Put deodorant in your locker.

7. Use mouthwash.

8. <u>Get on a sports team!</u>

Don'ts

1. Carry your books in front. Only girls do that.

2. Walk around like you're scared. Upperclassmen are like dogs—they sense fear.

3. Walk around like you own the school. You've got to know your place.

4. Talk to upperclassmen. Unless they talk to you first, in which case, answer them.

5. Sit by yourself in the cafeteria.

6. Talk about chitlins, fatback, or pigs' feet.

7. Bring your accordion to school—<u>ever</u>.

8. Look to me to get you out of any jams.

"Wuh-why . . . would I talk about chhhh-itlins? I hate chitlins."
Pig guts were one of Pops's favorites. Why, Melvin would never
understand. Whenever Mom cooked them, their house smelled like
the lake-cabin latrine for a week.

"Maybe you'd talk about how much you hate them. I'm just
saying, don't talk about them. White kids don't even know what
they are. And if they find out, they're going to think your family's
weird for eating them."

As far as Melvin was concerned, he wouldn't be talking about
anything in high school . . . because he wouldn't be talking. He
shrugged. Not because he didn't care what white kids thought. He
knew he did. *Shoot.* White kids made up practically the whole school.
If you didn't get along with *them*, you didn't get along at all.

Chuck crouched so they were eye-to-eye. "Look, I'm trying to help
you out . . ."

Melvin fixed on the last *Don't*: Chuck had said straight up not to
rely on him.

Don't worry, Chuck, Melvin thought, you're the last person I'd run
to for help. He set the list down and pretended to keep reading his
magazine.

"You've got to learn to speak up for yourself, Melvin. To stand up for
yourself. You're a runt who plays accordion, and then, with the stut—"

"I know!" Melvin shouted. Shouting routed the Stutter every time,
like a surprise attack. And he only played accordion because his mom
forced him to. He had no delusions of grandeur, but Mom was convinced he'd appear on television with his accordion one day.

"Easy now." Chuck gave him a cocked smile. He mock-punched
Melvin's shoulder, but Melvin shoved his hand away.

Chuck stood. "Like I said, I'm just trying to look out for you."

Melvin watched Chuck leave through the opposite door. No doubt going to swish some mouthwash—if it's been more than five minutes since the last time, Melvin thought.

He considered crumpling the paper with the *Dos and Don'ts* and using it to practice his shot. (Should he go out for basketball? He was way too short!!) Instead, he closed it inside his *Popular Science*. Then he rolled toward his Wall of Wonders, opened to chapter 1 of *Voice Power & Personal Power*, and got busy studying how to change his life.

CHAPTER TWO

omeone was shaking Melvin's shoulder so hard his teeth rattled in his head.

"Get up, Melvin! Get up!" It was Maisy.

He groaned and rolled over. He had planned to stay in bed as long as he could on this last Saturday of summer vacation.

Maisy's big eyes were wide with excitement. Her hair was freshly braided into two pigtails, and she wore the red-and-blue-checkered romper dress Mom had sewn for the first day of school. "I'm going to interview the baseball player." She held up her flip notebook, which she carried everywhere.

She scurried to the door. "I'll be outside writing interview questions. No lollygagging!" Maisy had picked up the unfortunate habit of using Mom's favorite word on the rest of them.

Had his eleven-year-old sister actually gotten a meeting with Spokane's newest minor league recruit? It was worth getting out of bed to find out.

Ten minutes later, Melvin slipped through the kitchen, grabbed an apple from the bowl on the dining table, and left through the back door, successfully avoiding Mom, Pops, and Marian. Chuck had been gone for a while already. Football practice at Cleveland had begun the week before.

Maisy jumped up from her spot on the back stoop. "Took you long enough!"

No comment. It was never worth trying to argue with Maisy.

"You should get your baseball mitt," she said. "Then he can sign it!"

He had already thought of that, of course, but he wasn't so sure it was a good idea. The last thing Melvin wanted was for a professional baseball player to think that he was slow—or worse, stupid—which he knew was what people thought when they heard him try to speak.

"Don't you *want* him to sign it?"

He shrugged, then nodded. Of course he did.

"Well, get it, then! Don't worry, Melvin, you know I can sweet-talk him into signing it for you." She grinned. She was right.

Pops always said it was better to be prepared and not have an opportunity than to have an opportunity and not be prepared. So, he headed for the garage, a small detached building, painted the same mustardy color as their house. He took in the soft smell of Pops's pink, yellow, and white flowers and the bright red blooms that exploded like fireworks alongside the garage. He could never remember the flowers' names, although Pops had tried to school him on them all.

He found his glove in the corner with the bats and balls, and stepped back out into the bright light. The Spokane sun was already so hot he felt like one of those three Bible men who got thrown into the furnace—Shadrach, Meshach, and Abednego.

They walked down the driveway and turned onto Empire Avenue, the street they'd lived on their entire lives. It was a wide, east-west thoroughfare with houses spaced evenly apart, their green lawns as neatly edged as Chuck's hair. Melvin knew who lived in each home they passed: Mr. Lamb had built the Robinsons' add-on so Marian and Maisy could have their own room. Mrs. Balducci and Mrs. Butler had brought casseroles when Mom was laid low with a bad illness. Mr. Berto and Pops swapped gardening tips.

There were a few trees along the street, but the standout was the giant ash in the Hatchetts' front yard at the end of their block. Melvin and Maisy liked to climb the tree with Jill and Dennis, the Hatchett kids. Sometimes, when they were feeling invincible, they would pluck the orange-red berries and drop them on unsuspecting passersby below.

Not this summer, Melvin thought. He was too old for that, and far from feeling invincible. They turned at the corner and headed toward Providence, Grandma Robinson's street. It was the perfect name, she said, because it was Divine Providence that had gotten her there.

Maisy bounced along, chattering about how she couldn't wait to write an article on the new baseball player—Will "the Cobbler" Thompson—and reciting all the questions she would ask. Why "the Cobbler"? Where had he lived before moving to Spokane? Why had he gotten into baseball? And what was it like, being the first Negro player for their city's minor league team?

"Our very own Jackie Robinson," Maisy exclaimed. "Living right across the street from Granny! Isn't it exciting, Melvin?"

He nodded. He never needed to say anything with Maisy. She understood how hard it was, which was one of the reasons Melvin liked being with her. She was also entertaining, and a big dreamer, which he admired. She was going to be Spokane's first paid Negro journalist, she said, just like the famous Ida B. Wells, and Melvin had no reason to doubt it. Maisy was going places.

They reached the pale green house that the whole Negro community had been talking about since the day Will Thompson had moved in. Was the Cobbler home now? A big blue Cadillac was parked out front.

Everything in Melvin from the neck up tightened, as if his mouth were one of those mechanical windup toys and someone was twisting the key. He'd been doing Mr. Feuchtinger's exercises faithfully for the past couple days, but so far they hadn't made a lick of difference.

Melvin glanced across the street to their grandma's place, a graying white house with one scrabbly evergreen tree in the front yard. Maybe they should pay her a visit first. She always had a cold bottle of fizzy ginger ale waiting for them.

Maisy flounced up the baseball player's front walkway in her checkered dress and knocked on the door.

Wait! Melvin wanted to shout. He needed to prepare himself. Maybe do a few of the tongue push-ups that Mr. Feuchtinger recommended for strengthening one's "vocal apparatus."

Too late. The door opened. Melvin's heart leapt into his throat, blocking his breath.

A man with bulging biceps, ebony skin, and conked hair—straightened with a wave put in it—stood in the doorway. His crooked nose looked as if it'd been broken, possibly more than once. Melvin recognized him right away as the man in the newspaper photographs, even without his baseball uniform.

"Can I help you kids with something?"

"Hello, Mr. Cobbler! I'm Maisy Robinson and this is my brother, Melvin. That's our grandma's house right there." She pointed across the street. The man's eyes followed. "We live not too far, and anyway, my brother here's a big fan. He even heard of you before you moved here. Said you were going to be the best thing that ever happened to Spokane's baseball club."

Melvin's face was heating up like a toaster the more she talked.

"Said you're like a celebrity person, like Nat King Cole or Marlon Brando or even Jackie Robinson, which is why I'd like to interview you. I'm a reporter for the highly respected and widely read newsletter of the Bethel A.M.E. Church, and I know for a fact that our readers would be very curious to know more about your many incredibly interesting life experiences."

The perfectly groomed, thin mustache that hugged the man's upper lip curved with his smile.

"And if you are willing, sir, Melvin here would like your autograph."

Melvin slowly moved his arm behind Maisy's back and pinched the skin on her upper arm.

She yelped. "What'd you do that for?"

Will Thompson's eyebrows rose almost to his conked hairline. "Listen, kid, I'm flattered. Really. But maybe you should let the boy speak for himself?"

"He's afraid to talk. Sometimes he acts like he's one of them mutants."

Melvin stomped on her foot for that. Didn't care *what* the man saw.

"I think you mean *mute*." The baseball player looked at Melvin. "You're obviously not deaf." Then he turned and went inside.

"Yyyyou're tuh-tuh-talking the mmmman's ear off!" Melvin shout-whispered.

Maisy blubbered something about being sorry, that she was just trying to cover for him since he wasn't saying anything, and in the end, it was his own dang fault because he wouldn't just stop caring about his stammer and talk to people.

The Cobbler came back with a ball and a pen. He scribbled on the ball, and then indicated with a flick of his head that Melvin should go long, which of course he did—scrambled down the steps and shoved his glove onto his hand as he jogged toward the sidewalk, nervousness flooding his chest. The Cobbler cocked his arm and lobbed the ball. It was headed straight for the pocket. Melvin could practically feel it, hear the deep, rich sound of it sinking into the leather.

Instead, it hit his glove with a *thud* and bounced off.

Melvin watched in horror as the ball descended toward the ground, landed on the sidewalk, and rolled away from his feet. He stared at his betraying glove in disbelief. All the strings had been removed.

Chuck!

Melvin would kill him.

He picked up the ball and ran.

CHAPTER THREE

y the time Melvin turned onto Empire Avenue he was huffing and puffing. He slowed his pace to a brisk stride. He was not hunting down Chuck to forgive him, no matter what Reverend Reed said about forgiving seventy times seven. He was going to give Chuck a piece of his mind. A *large* piece.

Mom, Pops, and Marian sat out on the front porch. It was how they all tried to stay cool, since the public pool had been made off-limits due to Mom's fear of the polio virus. Pops lounged in a low lawn chair with his straw hat over his face. Marian draped over one bent knee, putting that polish stuff on her toenails.

When Melvin turned up the walk, Mom stopped reading her *Jet*. She used the magazine to fan herself instead. "Where are you going in such a rush?" Mom's voice was high-pitched, like a flute. "And where's your sister?"

Melvin shook his head, even though he knew. She had stayed to ask the Cobbler her questions, while she had her chance. "Wwwwhere's *Chuck*?" He spat his brother's name, because he was mad, and to get it out quickly before the Stutter could stop him.

"Over at the North Pole, with a few of his football friends," Mom said.

Pops lifted his hat and looked out. "What you got there, son?"

Melvin lobbed Pops the ball, which he snatched in midair. Pops might have been slightly built, but he had a grip of steel. "Well, what do you know? You got yourself some real memorabilia here."

Maybe so, but the ball had been a side dish to a dinner-sized dose of humiliation. He turned and stalked away.

"Melvin James, where are you going?" Mom called.

"The North Pole!" he yelled, and kept on moving.

He would've liked to have kept walking all the way to the actual North Pole to get away from his embarrassment and this blasted heat and Cleveland High School and *all* of it, but the North Pole he was headed for was the local soda fountain at the major intersection east of their house. It was owned by the Hatchetts, the family with the ash tree. Melvin's family only ate there as a special treat, but lately, Chuck and Marian had been hanging out there a lot, spending their own cash from summer jobs.

With each step, Melvin got madder and madder. Chuck was always messing with him. Always trying to toughen him up. Always telling him it was for his own good—he was just "looking out for him." Chuck had often told Mom and Pops they needed to stop protecting Melvin so much. Well, he didn't need protecting. He could take care of his *own* self. And he was about to prove it to his brother.

A part of his conscience waved a hand, trying to get his attention: you know the glove was payback for how you got him in trouble with that girl the other day.

Chuck and one of the Carter girls, Arnetta, had been sitting on the porch, acting all goofy-like, and Melvin and Maisy had decided to have a little fun by calling out from the house that "Chuck's girl" was on the phone, at which point Arnetta had huffed and said she wanted him to take her home immediately. Chuck had been angry, but Melvin figured he'd been doing his brother a favor. Arnetta had been fawning all over him, and the last thing Chuck needed was more ego-stroking. If his head got any bigger it wasn't going to fit in his football helmet.

Melvin crossed busy Normandie Street and marched straight for the North Pole. He could see Chuck inside, sitting at a booth with his teammates, a whole gang of boys. *White* boys, Melvin noted. His throat tightened but he wasn't turning around now. He yanked open the door and strode inside, his glove lifted high.

Chuck grabbed his chest with one hand, pointed at Melvin with the other, and laughed. "What's wrong, little bro? Having some trouble with your glove?"

It's not funny! Melvin wanted to shout. But every time he opened his mouth, his words backed away like a kid afraid to jump off the high dive—running to the end and then stopping, over and over—until he could feel the pulsing of an artery in his forehead. His tongue felt as heavy and solid as a brick.

"Yuh-yooooo." You.

Took. Pulled. Messed. Broke.

Every word he could think of to describe what Chuck had done started with a sticky letter. He couldn't find a way around.

His mouth was like an idling motor in neutral gear. No matter how hard he tried, his words went nowhere.

Someone muttered behind him. "Yuh-yuh-yuh."

Melvin wanted to run but his feet had become slabs of stone. His face and palms prickled. He knew that voice.

Two guys from his class, Gary Ratliff ("the Rat" to Melvin) and Troy Odom, in practice jerseys and football pants, walked up with trays mounded with burgers, fries, and shakes—food for Chuck and his buddies. Most likely, the incoming freshmen were here to make good with the team's upperclassmen, doing whatever they were told in an attempt to be accepted into the club.

Gary spoke. "If it isn't Suh-Suh-Suh-Skip!"

He'd been calling Melvin "Skip" since the fifth grade. Skip. Like a needle on a record.

"You guh-guh-guh-going to eat with us, Sssskip?"

Chuck shot out of the booth like a bullet from a barrel before Melvin knew what was happening. Fries flew everywhere; the tray clattered on the ground; shakes splattered across the floor. Gary was on his back, his face doused in soda. A red welt bloomed under his eye.

Gary looked dazed. He sat up slowly, brushing fries off his front.

"Whoa, whoa, whoa!" Mr. Hatchett came out from the kitchen. "What's going on here?"

It was clear from the way Chuck was standing over Gary, his chest still rising and falling quickly, that he had been the one to push the Rat down.

"This crazy Negro attacked me," Gary said, moving quickly to get to his feet. He ran a hand through his blond hair, slicking it back in place.

"You know that's not the whole story," Chuck said through clenched teeth.

Melvin wanted to speak up, to come to his brother's defense, but his mouth was bound, and there was nothing he could do. He looked to Chuck's teammates, thinking surely one of them would say something. Their eyes were fixed on the table.

"Whatever the story is, it shouldn't have ended with you shoving this boy down. I'm surprised at you, Chuck. I think we both know your father wouldn't approve of this type of behavior. You are not those kind of Negroes."

Melvin smoldered watching Gary and Troy smirk behind Mr. Hatchett's back. If only he could knock those smug looks off their faces.

"Now apologize to this young man. Then I want you to clean up this mess you made."

Chuck's gaze remained down. He swallowed hard. Melvin felt his brother's humiliation like a boot on his own chest. Gary had been an arrogant brute as long as Melvin had known him, all the way back to first grade—when the Stutter had taken up residence in Melvin's mouth.

"Sorry," Chuck murmured. He looked at Gary piercingly. "And don't ever let me catch you making fun of my brother again."

"All right, that's enough." Mr. Hatchett held up his hands. "You Robinson boys clean up this mess, and then go on home. I'll get the mop." He handed Chuck a rag and went to the back.

Melvin stooped to pick up fries and put them on the tray. Chuck used the rag to wipe up the spilled ice cream.

Gary and Troy stood there awkwardly. Gary had made a fool of himself by mocking Melvin in front of Chuck's friends. Even though the other guys hadn't come to Chuck's defense, they made it clear with their body language that Gary was no longer welcome. He and Troy took off, but not before Gary shot daggers with his eyes at Melvin.

Melvin and Chuck cleaned in silence, while Chuck's teammates spoke in muted tones a few feet away. Melvin glanced Chuck's way several times, trying to get a read on how angry his brother was, but he never returned the look.

When they were finished, Chuck said goodbye to his friends. Melvin followed him out the door and they headed for home. "Next time," Chuck said, still not looking him in the face, "you're on your own." In spite of what he'd written in his *Dos and Don'ts* list, Chuck had gotten Melvin out of this jam, but now he'd made it plain: he was done stepping into the line of fire for his little bro.

Melvin wanted to talk to Chuck about what *else* had just happened, what they had heard Mr. Hatchett say. *Not those kind of Negroes.* It was as though the man were accusing them of something based on a completely backward set of laws. The words filled Melvin's chest with a dusky, slippery feeling that he couldn't get a handle on, let alone name. He wanted to expel the feeling, to push it away, but instead it seemed as if it were filling the spaces around his heart and lungs like thick smoke, making it hard to breathe.

Clearly, Chuck wasn't in the mood for talking. He stalked ahead of Melvin by a few paces.

Melvin's thoughts returned to Gary and Troy. Gary had been knocked down a peg in front of the older football players, but it wasn't the upperclassmen who he'd be taking his anger out on. Melvin's stomach suddenly felt like it was in the North Pole's milkshake maker.

He was entering Cleveland High with a traitor mouth and absolutely nothing standing between him and the Rat.

CHAPTER FOUR

elvin lugged their brand-new steel Coleman ice chest down the back steps. What was Mom bringing to the Jessups' annual Labor Day cookout—*bowling balls*? He set the chest on the ground to rest his arms and catch his breath.

Pops was in the driveway polishing the hood of his always pristine, pinkish-tan, Plymouth station wagon. The car was Pops's pride and joy. Sometimes he acted like it was his first child—or his second wife. Called it Big Bertha just to get under Mom's skin. When he could see his reflection in the *metal* side of the side mirror, that's when it was clean enough. Melvin's chore was to wash the behemoth every weekend. He had to stand on a stepladder to reach its black top.

Melvin tapped his leg, quick and surreptitious. It was a trick he'd learned over time: the movement distracted his brain just long enough to get his first words out. And if he could do that, the rest often flowed better. *Tap-tap-tap.* "Where do you wwwwant me to put the ice chest?"

Pops stood upright and gave his back a little stretch. "Bring it around here. Been waiting to set that in first."

Melvin strained to lift the thing. Pops chuckled. "It's a beast, ain't it?" He came over and took the handle on one end.

Melvin jerked his head, another tactic. "Thhh-anks."

"Mother insisted," Pops said. "Said every family in America's going to have a portable fridge soon, so we needed one too. I'm thinking it's going to be sitting in the garage most of the year." They moved around to the back of the station wagon. "Careful now. Don't scratch the paint."

They loaded it into the back and Pops went to work putting in the rest of their picnic paraphernalia. Blankets, baseball equipment, the croquet set. The large, red-and-white model airplane with the gas-operated motor he and Pops had built over the summer waited on the short green lawn. Its maiden voyage would be over the Jessups' country property. Melvin handed Pops what he asked for, and Pops placed things piece by piece, as he did with the jigsaw puzzles he was always putting together.

Pops liked order, which was probably why he'd ended up a postal worker, sorting mail. Back when he'd ridden the mail train to Montana, he'd shown Melvin, then seven or eight, how to use the "sorting box"—a wooden tray with sections that he'd slip mail into based on postal zone. Melvin would time Pops to see how fast he could sort a stack of envelopes with different addresses on them. Then Melvin would take a turn. He got pretty fast, but never as fast as Pops.

"You don't have to do things quick, Melvin," Pops would say. "Slow and steady wins the race." Even then, Melvin knew his dad wasn't talking about sorting mail. He was telling him, without saying so, to slow down his speaking.

Mom explicitly told Melvin to slow down when he was sticking on a word. Slowing down was her big solution. What she and Pops didn't understand was that it didn't make a difference. *No one* understood, because somehow Melvin was the only one in their family who had been cursed with this particular problem. In fact, he didn't know a single person who had to contend with a broken tongue.

As if he could read Melvin's thoughts, Pops said, "Seems like you're having a little more trouble with your speech these days, son."

Melvin handed him the last folding chair, avoiding his eyes. Every word felt like a fence too high to clear; if he spoke, his tongue would get snagged and he would fall on his face. So, he shrugged.

"You know your mom. She's worried, wanted me to ask you about it. I know going to where there are lots of people—even if it's all *our* people—might not be your idea of a good time, but as far as I'm concerned you don't have to talk at all if you don't want to."

Melvin appreciated what Pops was saying, but it also brought back up a question he'd thought before: Did he embarrass his dad?

"Only one thing left to load." Pops motioned to the plane. They'd spent many a day in the basement (which was nice because it was cooler), working contentedly in side-by-side silence. Melvin stooped to pick it up. It was lighter than one might think, because it was made of balsa wood, but its size made it awkward, and it could be damaged easily. They stowed it carefully on top of everything else. "You thought of a name yet?"

Melvin shook his head. "Mmmmmaybe something with *mmmm-majesty* in it?"

Something like *Millie's Majesty*, he thought.

Pops nodded. "Well, it's yours to name. You just let me know and we'll paint it on the side."

When everyone was ready to go, and not a moment before, Melvin slid into the back next to Maisy. Thankfully, Mom had allowed him to wear shorts, but that meant his legs would be sticking to the white leather car seat within seconds. If the ice chest was a portable fridge, the Plymouth was a traveling oven. Mom and Marian got in front next to Pops, and Chuck stuffed himself into the spot next to Melvin. The strong menthol smell of his Skin Bracer aftershave made Melvin's eyes water. He jerked his head. "Wwwhy you got to wwwwear that stuh-stuff, anyway?"

"You'll understand one day, Babyface." Chuck ran his fingers over Melvin's cheek before Melvin could stop him. Melvin had started checking his face daily for signs of manhood. So far, nothing. Not a single hair. Which was fine, for now, because shaving looked like a pain in the neck, but he also wanted Chuck to stop treating him like a child, and having a few chin hairs might force his whole family to recognize that he was growing up too. Not to mention Millie Takazawa . . .

They drove past her house, across the street and a few homes down from their own. It was small and white, with a cherry tree out front, and three green-painted steps leading up to the front door. The front door that Melvin had never had the courage to go and knock on, as many times as he had daydreamed about it from his own porch.

The Takazawas were a Japanese family known in the neighborhood for their small grocery, not far from the North Pole on Normandie. Mom bought fruits and vegetables there, and Melvin had been called on many a time to run down the street to pick up some eggs or milk if they ran out before the dairyman's delivery. He would often see Millie there, but usually only two words passed between them: *hello* and *goodbye*.

The car lumbered on. Maisy babbled about who she would interview at the cookout for the Bethel A.M.E. newsletter. Chuck looked out the window. Melvin pretended to listen to his sister, but really he was trying to bury his thoughts about starting high school (*tomorrow!*) by thinking about barbecued ribs and hanging out with Bubba.

They were headed to the Jessups' large home—large because they had six kids—north of the city. Their fourth kid, Bubba (whose real name was Francis, but God help you if you ever called him that), was Melvin's best friend. Like the Robinsons, the Jessups didn't live on the east side, where most of Spokane's Negro families dwelled and the two main Negro churches—Calvary Baptist and Bethel A.M.E.— had their buildings. They lived out in the country.

The Jessups were different in another way too. They were Catholic, which didn't make any difference to Melvin, except that it meant he and Bubba wouldn't be going to the same high school. Bubba would be continuing at St. Xavier's, the Catholic school. Melvin had been praying all summer for Bubba's conversion to a new religion.

Pops turned the car onto the long, dirt driveway that led to the two-story country house. Loads of people were already there, hanging out in small groups on the wraparound porch and in the backyard. Pops pulled into a space on the yellowed front lawn.

Mr. Jessup greeted them with a raised hand and a loud, "If it isn't the Robinsons!" He had the stature of a grizzly bear but his heart was pure Teddy. He was always dressed in a suit, and his lips held a pipe so often that it seemed like a feature of his face. Today was no exception—to the suit *or* the pipe—although on cookout days he left off the jacket, revealing his suspenders and rolled-up sleeves. Pipe smoke mingled with the dusty smells kicked up by the car's white sidewall wheels. Melvin knew what he'd be doing when they got home—washing Big Bertha.

"Careful there!" Mr. Jessup called out, waving his pipe. "Gonna set my grass on fire with the sparks coming off the underside of that low-riding Plymouth!"

"Maybe you should be a respectable neighbor and water your yard!" Pops yelled out the window.

Mr. Jessup looked around, wide-eyed. "Neighbor? Nearest neighbor be so far off they're not caring about my yard. There's a reason I live out here."

Pops got out and he and Mr. Jessup shook hands. "I'm a misanthrope, remember?" Mr. Jessup said.

Maisy leaned into Melvin. "What'd he call himself?"

Melvin knew what the word was, and even what it meant, but he didn't feel like making the effort and *M* words were some of the worst, which really stunk when your name was Melvin.

"Misanthrope," Marian said, sounding superior from the first syllable. "Someone who doesn't like people." Marian prided herself on her vocabulary. She was a member of the Paul Laurence Dunbar Literary Circle, named after a famous Negro writer, and formed by the Order of the Eastern Star, a civic group Mom was in. The Order, of which Mrs. Jessup was the president, had already committed a college scholarship to Marian, who would be graduating this year.

"But Mr. Jessup *loves* people!" Maisy exclaimed.

"They're just acting the fool," Mom said. "*Already.*"

Maisy had flipped open her notebook. "*M-i-s* . . . What's next?"

Melvin hustled out of the car, not wanting to stammer through spelling the word. Besides, Marian was already on it.

26

Pops removed their model plane. Chuck grabbed an armload of stuff from the car and headed toward the large back lawn. Melvin stared at the ice chest, knowing he'd make a fool of himself if he tried to carry it alone. Just in time, Bubba appeared, walking down the dirt driveway.

"Hello, Mrs. Robinson," he said, leaning down to kiss Mom on the cheek. Bubba was already as tall as his dad, and had the same Teddy heart. He greeted Marian and Maisy, as well, but saved the biggest grin for Melvin. "Hey, Melvin! How's it goin'?" They grabbed ahold of each other's right hands and moved in for a chest bump, slap on the back—an acceptable hug among young men. Between the Jessups' summer road trip to see family in California and the Robinsons' annual trek to Curlew Lake, Melvin hadn't seen his best friend the whole summer.

Exhale . . . ease in with an *H* . . . "Hhhhhow ya doin'?" Melvin was afraid if he attempted his friend's name all those *B* sounds would never stop, like an extra-bouncy rubber ball.

"Been good. Been *real* good." He leaned down and lowered his voice. "Got myself a girl. In Los Angeles. We've been writing back and forth."

Melvin nodded enthusiastically, even though he could feel the plaster in his smile. This was no good. No good at all. Bubba had hopped the train to *Lovesville*. He would leave Melvin on the side of the tracks. They each grabbed a handle of the gargantuan ice chest, heaved it out of the car, and started up to the house.

"Name's Franceda, and *woo-ee!* She's as pretty as her name."

Sounds kinda like Francis, Melvin thought, but he didn't point out the similarity between the girl's and Bubba's names. One, he didn't want a punch in the arm, and two, he didn't want to encourage Bubba to think that this was a match made in heaven, like Melvin's parents—Claude and Claudine—always called themselves when they talked about their suitably paired names. Bubba waxed on about how he and Franceda had met and the girl's many fine attributes.

Mrs. Jessup directed the flow of incomers like airplane traffic control. She was tall, with a thick neck and a commanding voice. They set the chest where she pointed.

If it were up to Melvin, they would hang out in Bubba's room until chow time—less need to converse—but Mrs. Jessup told Bubba to refill the half barrel of ice with more bottles of Coca-Cola and pass them around.

The first circle of men they approached included Pops and Mr. Jessup, along with Mr. Strong and Mr. Blackwell, who co-owned an auto repair shop. These three men were Pops's golf and hunting buddies. With them were Mr. Freeman, who operated a laundromat, and Mr. Pierce, who Melvin sang with in the Bethel A.M.E. choir. He was balding and had glasses as thick as Coke bottles, which made his eyes unnaturally large. All of the men wore slacks and short sleeves, not T-shirts, but collared button-ups, just a notch below church clothes.

Mr. Freeman was speaking when Melvin and Bubba walked up. "You should stop accepting them white people's business. They tryin' to barter you down 'til they be paying less than the cost of the parts you puttin' in their cars!"

"Only some of 'em," Mr. Strong said. His voice still had a touch of the Texas drawl he came with when he rode the trains to Washington State. He was tall and dignified.

Mr. Blackwell nodded. He was shorter and his glossy, rich brown skin reminded Melvin of the kukui-nut necklace Uncle Toussaint had brought Melvin from Hawaii. "Fact of the matter is, we rely on their business to stay open. Even if every Negro in this town brought us his car to service, there's not enough to keep us going."

"Not enough Negroes, or not enough Negroes with cars?" Pops asked. He looked knowingly around the circle.

"What's the difference?" Mr. Strong laughed sharply.

"I'm pretty sure any of us with cars is right here in my backyard!" Mr. Jessup said. The men guffawed.

"Excuse me, sirs," Bubba said. Melvin, and every kid he'd ever known, had been taught since birth that you were never to interrupt adults while they were talking, and if there ever was a break in the conversation (which it sometimes seemed like there never would be), you must always start with "Excuse me" and show the utmost politeness and respect. Unless you *liked* the feeling of a switch on your behind.

"Would any of you like a cool, refreshing drink?" Bubba and Melvin lifted the half barrel by its handles and the men chose their sodas, tipping their heads in thanks and going right back to their banter.

Melvin and Bubba made the rounds, with the unspoken understanding that Bubba would do all the talking. The Dalberts and Purcells, who played bridge with Mom and Pops every week, stood together. Mrs. Dalbert wore a gauzy light-blue dress and a white straw hat with pink flowers—*all-the-way* church clothes. Mr. Dalbert spoke directly to Melvin, which meant it would be rude for him not to respond: "Tell your brother we'll be at all his games, rooting him on."

Big year for him, now that he's a junior. College scouts will be watching."

Melvin mumbled, "Yyyessir."

"And also," Mrs. Dalbert said, her eyes shining. "Let him know that Eugenia is available for the Homecoming Dance."

Melvin and Bubba glanced at each other a moment too soon. They sputtered and turned away, but Melvin, unable to control his laughter or match Bubba's strength, lost his grip on the barrel. Ice and pop bottles crashed to the grass, splattering the four adults with cold water.

The two ladies shrieked. The men scowled.

"Sssssorry," Melvin forced out, although he wouldn't mind one bit if someone splashed *him* with icy cold water on such a scorcher. He scooped ice back into the barrel, while Bubba ran to the house for something to dry off the ladies. Mrs. Dalbert muttered about her expensive chiffon. Bubba returned with a dish towel, and the ladies swiped at their dresses. Melvin kept his eyes down until the foursome had moved on.

"Gonna tell your brother his wife's been picked out for him?" Bubba asked. They laughed out loud then, and made cracks about Chuck and his love affair with his own muscles until everything was back in the barrel.

They might as well have left it all on the ground, since someone called out not half a minute later, "The Carters are coming! The Carters are coming!" and the family (with their *fourteen* kids!) swarmed into the yard. The Carter kids were like locusts. As Grandma would've said (if she were at the Jessups' instead of cooking for rich white people at the fancy Spokane Club), the pop was snatched up "faster than you can say *Jack Robinson*." It was Grandma's favorite phrase because it included their family name.

Bubba and Melvin took the empty barrel as a sign that they had completed their duty and were about to go inside when Mr. Jessup whistled loudly. Time to eat. *Finally!*

Everyone gathered around, careful not to step on or accidentally kick any croquet balls, since some of the adults and kids were in the midst of a fierce competition. Mr. Jessup welcomed them all, and then Mrs. Jessup had an announcement. "This year, I've asked Miss Marian Robinson—member of the Cleveland High School's Treble Triad singing group, band majorette, and most likely (certainly most *deserving*) to win her school's title of Homecoming Queen—"

At this, everyone murmured excitedly. Spokane had never had a Negro Homecoming Queen.

"—to sing the blessing. Marian?"

Melvin's stomach rumbled so loudly, it set Bubba's younger brothers, Ant-Ant and Mikey, to laughing. One fierce look from Mrs. Jessup got that under control real quick.

The crowd stood reverently. Some with bowed heads and clasped hands. Others with eyes closed, faces upraised. Every shade of brown.

Marian sang: "Amazing grace, how sweet the sound . . ." Her voice was so rich, it was as if she were serving up sweet potato pie.

What happened, Melvin?

Uncle Toussaint's slurred speech slipped into Melvin's thoughts.

Seems that when God was handing out talents, He done gone and skipped right over you and me.

It was something Melvin had tried many times to forget. Uncle T hadn't been in his right mind when he'd said it. But the words clung to Melvin like the burrs he'd pick up on his socks when he forged through the tall grasses at Curlew Lake.

Marian, the talented performer and sophisticated socialite. Chuck, the popular athlete-leader. Both of them good at school and liked by all. And then there was him—incoming freshman whom teachers would be expecting to be just like his older siblings—and what did he have? The Stutter that wouldn't let him be.

What if it never went away?

His stomach clenched. Yes, he was hungry, but this was something more. Something that gnawed its way upward into the neighborhood of his heart. What *had* happened? What was wrong with him?

Later, when everyone's bellies were taut with ribs, collards, blackberry cobbler, and Mom's bottomless potato salad, the airplane Melvin had helped to construct awed the crowd with its impressive wingspan, buzzing engine, and ultralong-distance flight.

When Melvin, Bubba, Maisy, and Ant-Ant went to retrieve the plane from where it had finally gone down, however, all Melvin saw was its broken wing.

CHAPTER FIVE

The next morning, Chuck took so long in the bathroom Melvin barely had any time to himself in there. He needed to do his tongue exercises, and Mr. Feuchtinger recommended looking in a mirror to ensure they were being done correctly.

Chuck pounded on the door, saying he needed back in. He'd forgotten something.

"Yuh-you hhhhad your tuh-tuh-tuh-*time*!" The heat in his face rose. Stupid mouth. How would he make it through this day?

"Come on, we can both be in there," Chuck said. "I'm junior class president, Melvin. I can't be late."

Melvin rolled his eyes and opened the door. It wasn't worth starting World War III over.

Chuck grabbed the gigantic bottle of mouthwash under the sink. The bottle was so big not even Nikita Khrushchev could've used it up in a year. (He didn't know why, but Melvin imagined the Soviet leader having funky breath.) Chuck, on the other hand, would fly through it in a couple of weeks. His eyebrows jumped in time with his swishing. His cheeks puffed in and out. He looked like a deranged squirrel with a mouthful of nuts.

Maisy came in to brush her teeth. Three was definitely a crowd in that tiny space. Melvin slipped out behind them.

"Two minutes, Melvin," Chuck said, smoothing his hair in the mirror.

The butterflies in Melvin's stomach turned into bats, banging around so that it was hard to breathe. In less than an hour, he'd be walking the halls of Cleveland High, around all these kids he didn't know, having to speak up in class. And then there were the girls . . . He'd seen some of Marian's friends. They looked more like *women* than girls.

He went to his and Chuck's desk and opened the drawer that was his, on the left, since he was left-handed. He reached into the back of the drawer and searched with his fingertips until he felt the coolness of stone. He grasped the small sculpture—a small, carved turtle that she had given him in first grade.

Millie. He would never forget that day.

Mrs. Pleasant, their teacher, had read *Little Black Sambo* to the class. It was a story about a brown-skinned boy who outsmarted some tigers, turned them into butter, and ate them on his pancakes. Melvin had liked how the boy got one over on the tigers, and thought it was a good story. What wasn't good was how some of the kids had started calling him—the only little black boy in class—Sambo. It had made him feel different, as if his skin were emitting radiation and others didn't want to get too close.

After school, he'd told his mom. As soon as she heard, she marched to the school and had it out with Mrs. Pleasant and the principal, who agreed to have the book removed from their classroom. But that didn't stop the other children from calling him Sambo.

Sometime after that, the Stutter had shown up.

One day, in the midst of feeling marked and then, on top of that, helpless and dumb because he couldn't speak like everyone else, he arrived at his desk to find a small, shiny turtle with a brownish-green shell, black head, and black legs.

Millie's glances and shy smile made it clear: the turtle was from her. A token of her kindness.

He had tried to talk to her now and again, but she was quiet and he couldn't talk very well, and so they had never really spoken, even though they lived on the same street.

Chuck passed through their room, grabbing his letterman's sweater from the bedpost. "Come on. We can't be late!"

Melvin shoved the turtle in his pocket and followed.

In the dining area, a cloud of hair spray surrounded Marian's head, to keep her perfectly pressed hair in place. Melvin caught a whiff and coughed. The stuff was noxious. Mom put the lid back on the gold Spray Net can.

Maisy appeared from her and Marian's bedroom. She reached out to touch Marian's hair. "Ooooo . . . it's so poufy!"

Marian swatted her hand away. "No touching. It has to last all day."

"Sorry." Maisy looked genuinely remorseful.

Marian and Chuck said goodbye and left through the back door.

Maisy threw her arms around Melvin's waist. "I'm going to miss you!" she wailed. Maisy had three more years at Longfellow, the school where Melvin had spent the last eight years, and where he wished he were going that morning—*without* Gary Ratliff, who had made a practice of cornering Melvin at recess and commanding him to speak, so he and his buddies could laugh as Melvin struggled to get his words out.

"Off you go, now." Mom held out her hand. He took it, and she planted a kiss on his forehead.

He almost complained, but he didn't. He didn't swipe at the slightly damp spot where her lips had been, either. Not only because he didn't want to hurt her feelings, but because he wanted it to be magic. Who could say? Maybe a mom's kiss transformed on a kid's face and became a protective charm. And he could use all the help he could get. He felt like a sheep being sent off to a school of eight hundred wolves.

"I'm talking to the Lord about you every day . . . Prayer *works*, Melvin. You might not think so, but I know it does. So don't you worry none, you hear . . ."

He wasn't sure if he looked worried, but he sure *felt* worried. He had barely eaten anything that morning. He'd dumped his Cream of Wheat down the drain when no one was looking. Wasting food was up there with thievery when it came to Pops's version of the Ten Commandments.

Maisy gave him another bear hug.

He stepped outside just as Chuck yelled, "Melvin!"

They were already to the sidewalk. Melvin quick-stepped down the driveway.

"Just because I'm class president doesn't mean I can get you out of trouble if you're late."

How many times over this next year did he plan to mention his president status?

Chuck strode, straight and tall, looking like a . . . well, like a president on his way to an important meeting. A president cradling a football. His letterman's sweater was dark gray with orange trim and a large orange *C* on the front, which stood for *Cleveland*, of course, but charmingly matched his first initial. If Chuck was anything, he was charming.

Marian twirled her baton as she tripped along. She wore a white short-sleeved blouse with a rounded collar; a turquoise-and-blue plaid felt skirt; and a turquoise scarf tied smartly around her neck. The crinoline under her full skirt caused it to sway with each step of her brown penny loafers. Instead of pennies in the shoes' front slots, she had placed dimes, in case she ever needed to call home.

Melvin ambled behind them. They reached the Empire-Normandie intersection, where the library sat on the corner closest to their house, under a siren tower that went off every week to make sure it worked. The siren would warn them should the Soviets decide to carry out their threat to send over a bomb. The library was small and didn't have a whole lot of books, but it had atlases, and that's what mattered to Melvin. He'd pored over every single one, gathering facts and images of all the places he would one day see in person.

They crossed Normandie and passed the North Pole, not yet open for the day. Remembering their run-in with Gary caused Melvin's fear and worry to solidify in his stomach like a huge, hardened lump of Cream of Wheat. What would he do when he saw the Rat? He would avoid him as long as possible, of course. The whole school year, if he could.

Marian's friend Darlene met them on the sidewalk a few blocks later and the girls took up chatting, Marian never once breaking her baton twirl.

Melvin caught up to Chuck because he didn't want to listen to any more talk about which girl liked which boy and who had gone out on dates over the summer. Not the 45 rpm record he wanted on repeat. He and Chuck walked in silence. Melvin's shiny black shoes slapped the pavement. His feet felt huge. Mom always got their back-to-school shoes a size too big so they'd last the whole year and possibly into the next.

When the big brick building came into view, Melvin's mouth got so dry it felt as if he'd been eating chalk.

"Remember," Chuck said. "You're a square."

And you're obtuse, Melvin thought. Was his brother *trying* to be insensitive?

"Don't get stuck with another square." He spun his football in the air and caught it. "You can be a new man at Cleveland. Have a whole new image. Don't blow it, Melvin."

Chuck was serving up some Grade A guidance this morning. They reached the school. Melvin's eyes traveled up the side of the imposing two-story building. Chuck bumped his shoulder and kept on walking. "See ya, little bro. Good luck."

"Come to the field after school," Marian said to Melvin, not bothering to stop. "I'll be there . . ." She and Darlene saw some other girls they knew. They took off squealing, like two stock cars at Mead Race Track.

Melvin stared up at the school's brick front. *Grover Cleveland High School* was imprinted in concrete over the large, wooden double doors. Mom's uncle, whose house was the gathering spot for listening to boxing matches, was Grover Cleveland Harris. He was a good enough guy. Grover Cleveland, the president, had signed the bill that admitted Washington State to the Union. Neither fact made Melvin feel any better about walking through those doors. He stayed put on the sidewalk.

He was like a boulder in the middle of the rushing Spokane River. Kids—big kids—streamed around him. He didn't move. People knocked into him and kept going, just like the current. They'd all go inside the building and he'd be stuck to that spot, facing the doors.

His shirt chafed his neck. Marian had ironed it with so much starch, if he disappeared the shirt would still be standing there, like the Invisible Man. He sure did wish he *could* disappear. Every now and then, he caught a whiff of flowery perfume or that Spray Net stuff. Starch for hair, he thought, and laughed at his own joke.

Melvin became aware that he was being watched. A white boy smiled at him from the flagpole. Melvin gave the boy a once-over. His wavy dark hair was parted on the side and slicked down, but you could tell: *that* coarse hair didn't want to be slicked.

The boy was only a little taller than Melvin and a couple inches wider. He wore a buttoned-up suit jacket—only the third suit coat Melvin had seen out of all these kids—and outrageous black-and-white wingtip shoes. Who did he think he was? A nightclub singer? He carried a large orangish-brown case, as if he had packed clothes for a week. And he wore glasses. Black-framed, rectangular glasses.

This guy had *square* written all *over* him—and he was headed straight for Melvin.

It was exactly what Melvin needed to get unstuck. He turned from rock to water and joined the flow of the other kids, all the way through the giant front doors.

CHAPTER SIX

The linoleum floors were polished to a gloss so intense Melvin was afraid his shoes might shoot out from under him. It smelled like artificial pine and ammonia, with just a hint of lemon, like one of Pops's highballs, a "mixed drink" he sometimes enjoyed after work while sitting in his armchair.

Lockers lined the hall, interrupted every thirty feet or so by wooden doors with glass windows. He had memorized his class schedule and room numbers, and had practiced saying his teachers' names over and over, trying to get his mouth to like them.

For words that started with sticky letters, like B, C, L, M, N, P, S, T, and W, he found replacements whenever he could. But names were names. You couldn't change a person's name. Calling his teachers *ma'am* and *sir* wasn't much help—both started with sticky letters. And his homeroom teacher's name started with not just one but *two* sticky letters: Stimson. *If* he could get past the M of *Mrs.* first.

"Hey, Melvin!" Warren Hashbrook called out. Warren had been at Longfellow too. Melvin raised his hand to acknowledge him but kept on moving. *W* was a sticky letter and Warren was standing with a couple other guys Melvin didn't know.

He repeated his teacher's name silently as he got nearer to Room 23. He hoped the number was a good omen. Like Psalm 23. *The Lord is my shepherd; I shall not want* . . . He still felt like that lone sheep.

When he saw his homeroom, he slowed. He couldn't go in too early or he'd be breaking Chuck's *Do* number 2: *Be on time, never too early.* He'd kept the list in his magazine, and read it at least a couple dozen times. He moved out of the crush of students and pretended to be waiting for someone. He kept his head down.

Black-and-white wingtips stopped in front of his feet.

"I noticed you were laughing."

What kind of weird intro was that? The boy from the flagpole stood before him. The large leather case still hung from his side.

"Outside, you were laughing to yourself. I like a person who can laugh without anyone else needing to know what's funny."

The nightclub singer stuck out his hand. "I'm Lenny. Lenny Carini. Well, Friedman, actually, but Mom didn't want anyone giving me a hard time on account of us being Jewish, so we use her name instead of my dad's."

Melvin wondered how the boy's dad felt about that, but of course he wasn't going to ask.

"So, what was funny?" Lenny asked.

Melvin needed to think for a moment to remember that he'd even laughed to himself.

Starch for hair. He'd have to work around a lot of sticky letters to explain the joke.

He jerked his head. "Nuh-nothing, really." He was grateful the words slipped out without too much trouble.

Lenny shrugged. "And who are you?"

It was an interesting way to ask about someone you were meeting for the first time. There was so much Melvin could say. But he would stick with sharing his name. Or try, anyway.

He took a breath, relaxed his face, and hoped his mouth would go along with the program. "Mmmmmelvin." Not too bad.

"Nice to meet you, Melvin."

Melvin glanced into the classroom. Only two students sat at desks. Definitely too early to go in.

Lenny kept talking, but Melvin had stopped listening.

Millie was coming. Melvin ducked into the room (never mind the time) and made for a desk on the far side, near the windows. Lenny followed and sat at the desk next to him. This kid was more tenacious than the pine sap Melvin had to wash off Big Bertha every time Pops went hunting. Lenny's eyes flashed excitedly as he jabbered about how he couldn't wait for band class (turned out there was a saxophone, not clothes, in that case), where he'd gone to elementary, and then about his mother and the multitudinous ways she had embarrassed him in the ten minutes before he'd left for his first day of high school.

The boy could rival Maisy for number of words spoken per minute.

More students had trickled in, including Millie, whose entrance had set Melvin's heart to galloping. He glanced out the window to avoid staring. When he looked back, Millie was a few rows ahead and to the right.

He stared at the back of Millie's head, her shiny black hair curled and pinned up. She was so . . . serene. Like Curlew Lake at dawn.

When she looked over her shoulder at him, it was like a fish had leapt from the calm waters, startling, but amusing too.

He smiled. Her sparkling eyes were a reminder that there was a whole living, moving, breathing world below the surface of that quiet lake—that still, peaceful, calm exterior. She faced forward again, but the ripples caused by her glance, her shy smile, radiated toward him like little waves of joy.

Lenny leaned Melvin's way and whispered, "She'd be a real catch." He winked.

Melvin didn't acknowledge the comment. Instead, he glanced at the door, praying Gary Ratliff wouldn't walk in.

He looked around the room and tipped his head at Baron Carter, the only other Negro student besides himself. Melvin was used to it (and at the same time would never be used to it). He and his siblings had come to expect that it would always be just them in their classes—them and a Carter. With fourteen kids in the family, it was hard not to have at least one Carter in your class.

Right then he was more concerned about the Stutter than the color of his skin. How long would he be able to go without having to talk in front of everyone?

Mrs. Stimson sat behind her desk, hands folded. She looked like a lady from a Frigidaire ad. Housewifey, with her straw-colored hair poufed perfectly in place and a pleasant smile on her face. She rose from her desk and went to the door. Two stragglers made it through just before she shut it. Troy Odom—and Gary Ratliff. What was that his mom had said about prayer?

Gary's eyes narrowed when he saw Melvin. He and Troy sat directly behind him and Lenny. Of course.

There he was, a sitting duck-sheep. *In the presence of mine enemies* . . .

Mrs. Stimson introduced herself, welcomed them to their homeroom and social studies—"the study of human society"—and then said a bunch of other stuff. The only thing Melvin heard was that the majority of their grade would be based on classroom participation. She believed in "civic involvement" and the "power of democracy," and neither of these was possible without "vigorous dialogue and debate."

Class had barely started and already he knew he was done for. His stomach felt like it was being put through the wringer on Mom's washing machine. His legs jumped beneath his desk. If he didn't put his head down soon, he might black out.

Suddenly, it was time for the Pledge of Allegiance. Everyone around him stood. He had to stand. Stand up! he shouted at himself. But his legs wouldn't cooperate.

"You okay?" Lenny whispered.

"Young man," Mrs. Stimson called out.

Stand up, you fool!

Melvin felt Gary lean in. "Better stand up, Skip. Everyone will think you're unpatriotic."

Mrs. Stimson was walking toward their row. Melvin forced himself to his feet and pressed his hand over his heart. He teetered, but steadied himself with his free hand on his desk. Mrs. Stimson eyed him suspiciously but returned to her desk, where she began to recite the pledge. Kids droned around Melvin, while he silently mouthed the words.

"You cool?" Lenny asked again when it was over.

Melvin nodded. Then it was time for attendance.

To Melvin's chagrin, Mrs. Stimson required them to say "present" when she called their names. He sat in his seat, listening to everyone around him respond nonchalantly, with no effort whatsoever, while he was covered in sweat. He tried to keep his face as relaxed as possible.

Yea, though I walk through the valley of the shadow of death . . .

"Melvin Robinson," she called.

Lockjaw set in. He opened his lips in an attempt to vocalize, but nothing came out.

"Melvin Robinson?"

His heart pummeled his breastbone. His face felt like he was back out in the Spokane summer sun. His armpits were a swamp. He was melting on the spot, even more so because Millie was there, watching.

Kids who knew him from Longfellow craned to see where he was. Gary and Troy snickered. Lenny started to speak, but Melvin shook his head and scowled.

"His name is Skip," Gary said. "You know—like a needle on a record." He gave Troy a sly smile.

Melvin burned, remembering when Gary had once casually said—in his presence, of course—that a scratched record that skipped wasn't worth anything. You might as well just throw it away.

Mrs. Stimson looked back and forth between the boys, apparently waiting for someone to clear up the matter.

Melvin drummed his fingers furiously beneath his desk. He jerked his head. His face contorted with spasms.

"Mmmmmy nuh-nuh-*name* is Mmmmmelvin." The effort made his head spin. Anger burned in his stomach like acid.

"Thank you, Melvin," Mrs. Stimson said quietly, marking her book. She called a few more names. "Now then, everyone, sit up like you mean business and let's get started. It's time for another year of school."

CHAPTER SEVEN

elvin got through the rest of the day okay. He avoided having to speak in class, and when he wasn't in class, he was with Lenny, who talked as fast after the last bell as he had before the first.

"I know Miss Gale is pretty and all, but you sure you don't want to switch out of choir? We're going to have a hoppin' band this year!" Lenny's fingers wiggled madly in front of his chest, apparently practicing a wicked saxophone run.

Melvin removed books from his locker. Ever since he'd discovered at Bethel A.M.E. that singing broke the chokehold of the Stutter, he sang every chance he got. Besides talking to Tuck, it was the only time he could be certain his mouth would cooperate. So, no, he was not leaving choir. He shook his head.

"Sure? You already play an instrument."

Earlier in the day, Lenny had asked him straight out if he played anything. Melvin couldn't lie. He had copped to playing the accordion.

"It'd be easy to pick up another. How 'bout trumpet? Like Satchmo!" He held an imaginary horn in front of his mouth and pretended to blow. "Hey, what'd you think about Mr. Farber?" Lenny asked excitedly.

Their science teacher had impressed Melvin, for sure. He had a wooden arm with a hook, just like in the pirate books. It had been hard not to stare, but he used the hook so deftly that it quickly became like another implement in his science experiment, like pliers or tongs. He'd ended their day with a bang, literally, showing them how different gases responded to heat by holding a blowtorch to balloons filled with hydrogen, oxygen, nitrogen, and helium.

"I think he's going to be a real gas!" Lenny laughed. "When he told us he was part-machine—a product of modern science—and then he *took off his arm?* Whoa! I was hooked—so to speak." He guffawed. Lenny was really cracking himself up.

Melvin smiled in return. In spite of his earlier hesitations, he was finding himself liking this kid who slung words like a short-order cook. "Hhhhow do you think he llll-luh-lost his arm?"

"No idea. But I'd sure like to find out." Lenny's thick eyebrows rose and fell behind his glasses. "Hey, you should come over to my place. We could do homework, or better yet, have a jam session." He raised his instrument case.

Chuck's advice circled in Melvin's head like a ranch hand rounding up misguided thoughts that, according to Chuck, would lead him astray if they weren't reined in. He's a square! he could hear his brother say.

Melvin volleyed back. So what? I made a friend on the first day! If I stick with him, I won't walk the halls alone or wonder where to sit in the cafeteria this whole year. He and Lenny had the exact same schedule except for choir and band.

Melvin shut his locker as Millie walked by. He stared. He couldn't help it. Lenny bumped his arm. "Go talk to her."

Melvin had been imagining himself doing that very thing all day—but there was no way. Not now. Not without knowing what would happen when he opened his mouth.

Lenny pushed him in her direction. "Go! Give me a ring later and we'll figure out another day to hang out."

Melvin didn't have time to explain why phones and the plague were equally undesirable in his mind.

"You can thank me tomorrow." Lenny smiled slyly.

Melvin walked briskly, intending to catch Millie . . . or at least that's what he told himself. He followed her out the front doors and down the steps to the sidewalk. She scurried to a black sedan waiting at the curb. Mr. Takazawa sat in the driver's seat. He looked like a stone bust behind the steering wheel.

If he shouted her name he wouldn't stutter. He took a deep breath.

What will you say if she actually stops to talk?

His oversized shoe caught on a raised crack. He lurched forward; his books flew from his hand. He dropped to the ground to pick them up before the stampede of kids trampled them underfoot. Or before Millie noticed.

Someone passing by kicked his social studies textbook. It skittered across the concrete. The kicker loomed over him. Melvin didn't need to look up to know who it was.

"Second time in a week I've seen you down on your knees, Skip. Which is exactly where you belong." Gary laughed as he and Troy walked away.

Millie was gone, of course—whisked away like Cinderella in her carriage. He stared after her, but he was no prince. Squatting on the ground, watching everyone stream around him, he was a toad. A dumb croaking toad. He retrieved the last book and walked toward home.

When he got there, a red Chevrolet Bel Air with rear fins sat in the driveway. Uncle T? Uncle T mostly lived in Seattle, or somewhere on the other side of the state. He didn't come around but once in a blue moon. Mainly Thanksgiving, Christmas, and Easter—the eating holidays. Melvin took the front steps slowly. What was he about to walk into?

Pops, who worked five to two at the post office, sat stiffly in his black leather recliner. Uncle T sat on the couch.

"Little Mel, my man!" Uncle T stood to greet him.

Melvin shoved his free hand into his pants pocket and drummed his fingers like mad. "Hhhi, Uncle." He stopped there. The *T* was not going to come willingly.

"How you doin'?"

"Guh—" Melvin's face contorted as he tried once more.

He couldn't get it out. He could see it ("GOOD!") in neon green, flashing in his brain like the "OPEN" sign at the North Pole soda fountain, but he could not get his mouth to make the sounds that went with those letters.

"I hope you aren't about to say 'girls.'" Uncle T slapped him on the back as if he might dislodge the word. "You becoming a ladies' man, Little Mel?"

Time to change tactics. "I'm o-kuh-kuy-kay." He kept his face down, hoping Uncle T wouldn't see his shame.

"Hey, if you're nervous about going to Cleveland, don't be. You're named after a *war* hero. Can't nothing scare you, right?" He nudged Melvin with his elbow and winked. Had Melvin heard a little sarcasm when his uncle said "war hero"?

"Plus, you is mighty smart. Mighty Melvin, that's my man!" Uncle T wrapped his arm around Melvin's neck and scrubbed his head with his knuckles.

Mom came into the room from the kitchen. She gave Melvin a quick hug as he passed by. "You all right?" Her face showed her concern.

He nodded. Inside his room, he left the door ajar so he could hear their conversation.

"So, how much you asking for?" Pops said.

"Just enough to get me through the next few months."

"But how much exactly?"

Melvin's ears tuned in as if he were an operative picking up a transmission from the Soviet Union.

"A few hundred."

"A few hundred! I don't have that kind of cash lying around!"

"Come on, now. You have this house. And all these nice things. A TV, even. You take trips with your family."

"We take *one* trip a year to a lake with no amenities and modest accommodations. You telling Mama you're here this time?"

Silence. Melvin crept toward the door and listened at the opening.

"It's been six years," Pops went on. "Don't you think—"

He was talking about their brother's memorial, which had happened eight years after he died because it took that long to recover his body from the bottom of the Pacific Ocean. Sunk with the U.S.S. *Arizona* when the Japanese bombed Pearl Harbor. Uncle Melvin had been the first Negro to die in what became World War II. Not exactly the kind of "first" people aspired to, but still, he had been a hero to the Negro community in Spokane. Many had framed pictures of him in their homes for years after. And Melvin would always carry his memory . . . in his name.

Melvin remembered the funeral service vividly. It was where Uncle T had whispered that awful question: *What happened, Melvin?*

"Are you going to loan me the money or not?"

"Toussaint, you're my brother. I've looked out for you as much as I could. But you're on your own this time."

"Okay, *brother*. But I tell you what. You trying to live like the white man in this here neighborhood ain't gonna get you nowhere. Plus, it be puttin' pressure on young Melvin there."

"Now, Toussaint," Mom said quietly.

"Claudine, listen. Why you think that boy got that stammer? 'Cause he's surrounded by all these white folks, that's why. You shouldn't be here. Should be on the east side. Or do you think you're too good for that?"

"Leave," Pops commanded. "Now."

With that, the door opened and shut.

Melvin lay on his bunk. He stared at the world map overhead, places he would one day see in 3-D and living color, not flat pastels on paper. He traced the lines around countries in Asia, Europe, Africa. Lines that didn't actually exist, and yet still somehow kept people separate. Lines that made all the difference in the world.

Pops had crossed a line. Was Melvin suffering because of it, as Uncle T seemed to think?

Melvin didn't know. What he *did* know was that he'd made it through his first day. Just 179 more to go.

CHAPTER EIGHT

elvin was reading in his room when Chuck and Marian got home. High school was going to be a lot more work than elementary. He heard Chuck's duffel bag hit the living room floor.

"Pops, you're not gonna believe this!" His brother sounded angry. "Coach Harding benched me for the first game!"

Melvin had to see what was going on. Chuck paced the living room between Maisy and the turned-on television set Pops had brought home earlier that summer. It'd been the most exciting thing that had happened to the Robinsons in months, maybe years. Way more exciting than the Coleman portable icebox.

The sound of a crowd laughing came from the TV. "Melvin, turn that down, will you?" Pops said from his recliner.

Melvin found the volume knob and twisted it—the wrong way at first, which made them all jump at the loud sound. He spun it the other way and the actors were suddenly muted.

"What happened, now?" Pops chewed on the mouthpiece of his unlit pipe. No way would Mom ever let him light it in the house.

"Yeah, what happened?" Maisy said. Melvin half expected her to pull out her flip notebook and pencil.

"He's not being fair," Chuck said. "Punishing me and not even considering the other guy—who's a royal *jerk*, by the way."

Mom stood in the kitchen doorway. "Charles, please calm down and tell us what happened." Marian stood behind Mom, her face a stolid mask.

Chuck perched on the edge of the couch. "I was defending *him*." He pointed at Melvin.

Melvin's heart thudded.

"This punk freshman on the team made fun of Melvin, and I . . . I knocked him down—Saturday at the North Pole. I didn't tell you because, well, I didn't think it was a big deal. But apparently the kid's father said something to Coach and he's punishing me. Didn't even ask what the other kid did. Said it didn't matter. I'm supposed to set the example."

Pops sat silently, considering Chuck's situation. "Sounds about right to me."

Chuck glared at Melvin. "But two other guys on the team got into a fight, and he's not benching either of *them*."

"Two white boys?" Pops asked.

"Yes."

Pops's lips tightened around the pipe. He kept his eyes on the TV. Finally, he set the pipe on the table next to his armchair. "Got to learn how to restrain yourself, son, or someone will do it for you. And they definitely will not be fair about it. Most things about this country were never intended to be fair for us."

"Well, maybe *we* should do something about that."

"Doing it in my own way." Pops's gaze flicked toward Chuck, then back to the television.

Chuck exhaled audibly and stalked to their bedroom, bumping into Melvin on the way.

The comedy on TV suddenly seemed a lot more interesting than Melvin's social studies textbook. He'd let Chuck have the room to himself for a while.

* * *

The next few days, Melvin got through roll calls by clearing his throat real loud and raising his hand when the teachers looked up. He avoided being called on by keeping his eyes down. He was discovering that it was easy to be invisible when teachers didn't really want to see you anyway.

One teacher who refused to let Melvin hide was Mr. Farber. He would call on Melvin whether Melvin was looking at him or not. And Melvin for sure never raised his hand. He stuttered like crazy when he had to speak—about energy particles or electricity—but they were things he knew well from reading *Popular Science*, and things he was interested in. He felt the other kids' discomfort, but Mr. Farber didn't seem fazed and that helped.

Friday after school, Lenny tried yet again to get Melvin to come over so they could play their instruments together. They stood on the sidewalk. Kids talked and laughed around them. Some headed across the street to the Tiger's Den, the lunch counter where Cleveland students hung out after school. Lenny loosened his tie.

"I cuh-cuh-cuh-*can't*," Melvin said. Every time Lenny had asked, Melvin had come up with an excuse. This time it was that his grandma needed his help with something, which was true.

The main reason Melvin kept saying no was that it turned out Lenny lived in an apartment above the Harlem Club, which sounded cool except for one problem: Melvin's parents did not approve of the Harlem Club, for differing reasons. Mom, because she didn't agree with all the drinking that went on there and because the place was infamous for semi-regular brawls. Pops didn't like that the owner, a Negro man from down South, maintained a "whites only" policy five out of seven nights a week. "Even if it *is* an economic necessity," Pops would always add, "it's segregation, and it's not right."

Surprisingly, Lenny had lived there almost his whole life; his mom was the head cook.

"Okay, well, maybe this weekend. I'll call you!" Lenny raised his saxophone case in a parting gesture and they went their separate ways.

Melvin knew already—he wouldn't be available when Lenny rang. He didn't even take calls from Bubba. Phone conversations were Melvin's kryptonite. Talking on the phone . . . well, that was the problem—he *couldn't* talk on the phone. The Stutter made sure of that. Lenny would learn eventually, if he hung around long enough.

* * *

"What do you think Granny wants us to do?" Maisy scraped the toes of her Mary Janes on the steps leading to Grandma's door.

"Buh-better stop scraping." Pops blew a gasket whenever he saw Maisy's scraped-up shoes. He never stayed mad at her long, though. It was clear that Maisy was his favorite.

Grandma Robinson came to the door in her "housedress," made of thin cotton, with buttons down the front and two large pockets where she stuffed her tissues. Her fuzzy gray hair was pulled back in a bun, and she smelled faintly of wintergreen, because of the mints she liked to suck. "How're the king and queen of Empire Avenue this fine afternoon?"

"Marian's been nominated to be a *real* queen," Maisy reported.

"So I heard." Grandma led them through the front sitting room, through the kitchen, to the basement door. "Your mother called me earlier. Homecoming Queen—that's big news. You'll write an article for the newsletter, I assume?"

"Of course!"

"That's my girl."

Melvin eyed the refrigerator longingly.

"Ginger ales will be available for young bodies that work hard, once they are *through* for the day. And when you finish the whole job, there'll be three dollars apiece waiting for you."

Maisy's grin spread across her face. "Three whole dollars! We'll be rich, Melvin!"

Three dollars *could* buy him the new model airplane kit he'd been wanting, even if it wouldn't make them rich. Silly kid.

"What do you want us to do, Granny?" Maisy asked excitedly.

Grandma opened the door to the basement. "You're going to make me a fallout shelter." The rickety wooden stairs creaked under her weight.

Fallout shelter?

Melvin recalled the article in *Popular Science*. A basement wouldn't do you any good if you were in the blast zone, but it could protect you from fallout, if it was sealed up properly.

"Are the Russians really going to drop a bomb on us, Granny?" Maisy followed her down the steps. Melvin peered into the dank darkness. He'd only been in the basement a few times, to fetch a jar of stewed plums or mincemeat filling. And once to retrieve a baseball that had gone through a window. It had been his fault, but Chuck had taken the punishment with him, a decent big-brother thing to do.

A seam of light appeared around the cardboard-covered window. It had never been fixed. Not exactly radiation-proof.

"President Eisenhower and all his bigwigs out there in the other Washington been practicing getting out of the city as fast as they can. And I say if they're aiming to be ready, then we should be getting ready too." Grandma waded through boxes of stuff and pulled a string hanging from a single lightbulb, which clicked, then glowed yellow.

"It looks like a junkyard!" Maisy said.

There was barely room to walk across the packed dirt floor. Paint peeled from the concrete walls and the air smelled of damp cardboard and mildew. Wooden shelves held jars of various fruits and vegetables, which reminded Melvin of the animal specimens in formaldehyde that Mr. Farber kept in his classroom.

"After your great-grandma died, I went down to Peaceful Valley to see what I could save."

"It looks like you moved her whole house in here," Maisy said. She picked up something that looked to be part kitchen utensil and part torture device.

"Paper's been saying Spokane is a prime target," Grandma said. "We've got an air force base and an aluminum plant. But the government's not doing anything to keep us safe. Oh, *no!* We've got to get our *own* selves ready."

"Wwwwwhat do you want *us* to do?" Melvin was having one of his better days. Still, he felt dazed by the heaps of stuff surrounding them.

"I want you to use those smart brains of yours and figure out what to keep and what to throw away, and if anything can be sold, we'll split the money from selling it."

What here would be worth anything? It looked like piles of trash to Melvin. Boxes of church bulletins and piano music, phone books, and *PennySaver* newspapers. Piles of fabric—were those old dresses or curtains? A stack of bricks. Some broken-down chairs. Loads of empty jars.

"Why's that in here?" he asked, pointing to a car bench seat covered in tan fabric.

"Oh *that* silly thing. Some female singer Toussaint met when he was playing his trumpet at a jazz club in Seattle sat on it, so when he wrecked the car, he pulled out the seat and put it down here. Says one day when she's famous, he's going to sell it to a museum." Grandma let out a short hoot.

Melvin and Maisy exchanged looks. Then Melvin's eye landed on the weirdest piece of junk yet. Way in the far corner of the basement, set atop a wooden crate like a statue on a pedestal, was a *toilet!* Melvin pointed it out to Maisy.

"Did someone famous sit on that too?" she asked.

Melvin laughed.

"As a matter of fact . . ." Grandma pushed her way to the back of the basement.

"*What?!*" Maisy screeched. "Who?"

They followed in Grandma's wake, like explorers wading through a swamp.

"Louis Armstrong."

"*The* Louis Armstrong?" Maisy's eyes bugged.

Melvin gazed at the toilet in awe. *Satchmo.* Wait until he told Lenny.

"I suppose I can't say for certain that he *sat* on it. But he used it, all right. Back in the day when he first came through town, none of the fancy downtown hotels would allow him and his band to stay."

"What? *Why?*" Maisy asked.

Melvin didn't need to be told.

"Because they were colored," Grandma said matter-of-factly.

Maisy's lips pinched tight and she huffed through her nose.

"So *our* families took them in. After they performed, we had our own all-night after-party. We started over at Wally Harper's, where the toilet come from." Grandma gazed at the porcelain fixture, lost in her reverie.

"Ooo, I'll never forget," she went on. "When we got there, Wally didn't have nothing to serve but some Ritz Crackers and Spam. What an embarrassment!"

"Did you actually meet him?" Melvin asked. "Louis Armstrong?"

"Meet? Child, he was buzzing around me like a bee with a flower. We danced to more than a few songs."

Their grandma had mingled with the most famous trumpet player in the world! *Wow.* What other secrets might lie concealed in this junk pile of a basement?

Maisy's nose wrinkled. "So how'd you get the toilet?"

And *why?* Melvin wanted to know. It was a strange memento, even if a world-class performer had once graced it with his derriere.

"Well, Wally Harper was getting a new toilet put in, so I asked if I could have the old one."

"Because Mr. Armstrong used it?"

"Oh no, child. Because you never know when you might need a new toilet!" Grandma Robinson cackled. "Now, that's enough jawing. If you're going to finish this by the end of the weekend—"

"End of the weekend!" Maisy nearly shouted. "Granny, this might take us the whole school year."

"Oh, I don't know about that. But I *do* know the longer you wait, the longer it's going to take. Now, let's get moving."

Melvin spent the next two hours hauling stuff up the stairs and to the back alley. Grandma had apparently won over Will "the Cobbler" Thompson with lots of homemade fruit cobblers ("Believe it or not," Grandma said, "it's his favorite dessert!"), and he would help her by taking stuff to the dump. In return, she would let him use the fallout shelter, when the time came. And she was convinced it would.

Finally, Grandma called a break. She headed to her room to lie down "for a spell," while Melvin grabbed two cold ginger ales from the fridge, popped off their metal caps, and took a swig. He loved the sharp, spicy taste of the pop and the fizz on his tongue. It made his mouth feel tingly and energized and like he could say anything he wanted to without giving it a second thought. He took the drinks to the basement for him and Maisy to enjoy.

They had gotten a fair amount done. The mountains of junk were now small hills. Fifty percent more of the floor was visible than when they had arrived. Maisy sat on the tan car seat with a box on her lap. Melvin sat next to her, expecting her to grab a bottle and start guzzling, but whatever was in the box had her transfixed.

"Melvin, look at these—from when Daddy was a boy."

Melvin put the ginger ales on the ground and took a stack of photos. He'd never seen any pictures from Pops's childhood. They didn't have any at the house, so far as he knew. Pops was the eldest, but he had never been the largest. Standing next to his brothers, Pops looked scrawny!

Just like me, Melvin thought.

He sorted through the photos, looking for one of Pops around his age. He found a few: Pops holding a fishing pole. Pops sitting on the front steps of their home, a step above his brothers, who made silly faces while he looked on with a serious, big-brother, caretaker look. There was a larger photo of a baseball team. It was easy to find Pops—the only brown face in a group of white boys. All of them wore their old-timey, funny-looking baseball uniforms with belted baggy pants and lace-up leather ankle boots.

Melvin picked up a photo of Pops with his arm around the neck of a white boy. He looked like the same boy who was standing next to Pops in the team picture—dark hair slicked back from a high forehead, a long, skinny nose on a thin face, and ears that stuck out just a bit. In the photo of just the two of them, the boy's face was turned in slightly, like he'd been caught off guard by being embraced. He wore something like a beanie cap, but much smaller. Like one of Grandma's fancy teacup saucers, but solid black, turned over on the crown of his head. The most interesting thing was in the boy's hand: a silver goblet that looked like something out of a King Arthur legend.

Melvin flipped it over. No date or any writing on the back to say who it was. "Look at this one," he said to Maisy.

"Ooo, that's a fancy cup," Maisy said. "I wonder who the boy is."

Whoever he was, he and Pops were clearly more than just team-mates. The way Pops's arm draped over the boy's shoulders, they looked like true buddies.

Melvin put the picture back in the box, but the old images had opened the lid on a new thought: Pops had been young once too, with buddies, boyhood pleasures, and possibly an enemy or two. The only black boy in a sea of white faces. Had he been singled out at times? Or made fun of? It made Melvin wonder.

CHAPTER NINE

Melvin got through the next week of school by keeping his head down and staying focused on his two favorite classes: science and choir. In science, his knowledge had gained him respect among his classmates so that his stutter didn't matter so much, even to him. He actually raised his hand to be called on a few times. And in choir . . . in choir, Melvin let his voice soar! He loved every minute—every second—he got to be there, singing the sweet melody of "Blue Skies" or bellowing "My Country 'Tis of Thee." He felt like a normal kid in that room.

Friday came again. After school, Melvin and Lenny joined a crowd outside, watching and cheering as the football team and the marching band's upperclassmen loaded onto two buses, headed for Lewis and Clark High School. Chuck would get his first chance as a starting running back, and Marian would lead the band as majorette. Earlier, Melvin had wished them both luck.

The buses pulled away. "Finally!" Lenny exclaimed. "You get to meet the Thirteen Black Cats! I've told them all about you."

Lenny had worn down Melvin's resistance and so they were going to his home above the Harlem Club together. A surge of energy coursed through Melvin. The Thirteen Black Cats was the restaurant's house band. Every Harlem Club ad featured their "sizzling syncopation." They were famous—at least Spokane famous—and they knew about him!

Lenny had convinced Melvin to bring his accordion to school so they could go straight to the club. It was a breach of Chuck's *Don't* number 7, but he had stashed his case in the band room with the teacher's permission, and thankfully, no other kids had found out what was inside.

He nodded excitedly, to show Lenny he was also looking forward to it, although he had some worries. What if he choked in front of all those cool cats? Plus, the fact that he hadn't been completely forthright with his parents about his after-school destination pecked at his conscience.

"We are going to *jam!*" Lenny said.

Melvin's case bumped against his leg awkwardly as he walked. He didn't think he or his accordion could jam, cook, sizzle, or any other verb that made a person think about food. But if playing music with Lenny got him closer to a plate of the Harlem Club's famous chicken, he would try. "So, you've . . . lived at the—" *Club* was stuck in his throat. "At this puh-place your whole—" Stuck. Again.

"My whole life. Yep." Lenny had finished his sentence, which typically would have irritated Melvin, but didn't for some reason. Probably because Lenny treated him normally and not like he had some major handicap that made Lenny uncomfortable.

"Well, actually, we moved in when I was two. Ma had come out west from New York and she met my dad, who was in college at Gonzaga."

Lenny rarely spoke of his dad. Melvin's interest was piqued. He knew Gonzaga, of course, the local university Bubba planned to attend. Rollins Turner, a homegrown boxing champ, had recently become their first Negro law school graduate.

"I guess it was unusual for a Jewish boy to go to a Catholic school, but my mom says he didn't care about those kinds of things. He liked challenging the rules."

It made Melvin think of Pops. Is that what he'd been doing when he'd chosen to live in a different part of town? Challenging the rules?

"Anyway, after my dad died, Ma got a job at the club. Mr. and Mrs. Jones took us in, let us have room and board as part of her salary. I've spent my whole life hanging around that kitchen and dance floor."

Lenny's dad was dead. He'd said it so casually. Melvin wasn't sure what to say.

He didn't get a chance to say anything, because Lenny was off on another topic, telling him about Sulli, the sous-chef in the Harlem Club kitchen who'd taught him how to cook. Melvin watched Lenny out of the corner of his eye. Some part of Lenny was always moving, like a marionette. If it wasn't his mouth, it was his hands, feet, shoulders, eyes—skittering around like droplets of water on a hot iron skillet.

Grandma Robinson had once told Melvin he spoke like a baker, measuring everything carefully, decorating with a slow, steady hand. She said it was good that he didn't overdo it with his words, leaving big, tangled piles of icing everywhere. But sometimes— most of the time—he wished he could talk like Lenny was doing right then, saying whatever he wanted to, when he wanted to, the words flowing like frosting from a piping bag in the hands of a skilled pastry chef.

When they got to the club, the first thing Melvin noticed was the enormous sign on the roof. "Dine-DANCE" flashed in glowing letters, even at three-thirty in the afternoon. The words shared the giant *D*, so first you'd see only the "Dine," and then the "ANCE" would light up, inviting everyone for miles around to come and get their jitterbug on.

The sight and sound of that electric sign sent a current through Melvin's body. He quickened his step, his feet itchin' to start twitchin', and he didn't even like to dance. He buzzed with the excitement of being inside a place he'd only heard stories about.

Police raids during Prohibition. The occasional appearance of famous entertainers like Louis Armstrong and Nat King Cole. And of course, every night, the swing band, the Thirteen Black Cats, who kept the place bouncing and bopping.

"Is it tuh-true MMMMr. Jones's kuh-kuh . . . *kids* perform shows?"

"The younger ones still do, Little Butch and Delilah. They're really good. They do a Lindy routine that brings down the house every night. Between them and the Cats, the joint is always jumpin'!"

They approached the building, a single-story dance hall in need of a fresh coat of white paint. Four steps flanked by concrete posts and railings led to the door, which had a vertical row of small square windows on either side. The front of the building was dotted with shrubs. No great shakes, but then, Sterling Jones wasn't known for his landscaping. Only for providing a good time.

It wasn't nearly as grand as the Spokane Club, where Grandma worked, at least not on the outside. Melvin had never seen the inside of the Spokane Club, other than the kitchen, and to get *there* he had to go through the rear basement door, like Grandma and her coworkers. Only white people walked through the front doors.

"Cuh-can we . . . guh-go through the front?" Melvin asked, recalling Pops's complaint about this place and its practices.

"It's locked until doors open for dinner." Lenny motioned with his head. They walked around the side where a whole other building, attached but distinct, rose up two stories. Lenny pointed. "We live up there."

While they were looking, the electric sign on the building sparked, like a miniature fireworks display. The *D* flickered, then went back to radiating its flashing yellow glow.

"That old sign . . . Ma's been on Mr. Jones about replacing it for a while. Wonder when he's going to get around to it."

Melvin followed him through the side door and was smacked in the face with strong smells of cooking: cured ham, baked chicken, starchy steam from boiling potatoes, and a peppery-buttery mix of scents that warmed his nose and set his stomach to grumbling.

The club was known around town for its chicken plates, smoked spareribs slathered in famous "Come-Back" sauce, and Mrs. Jones's tongue-twisting, "Take-You-to-the-Sky" lemon meringue pie, which she brought to church picnics. Some folks said she was only advertising their business, trying to draw good churchgoers into that "devil's lair."

But the critics weren't only concerned about whether the club was an appropriate place for an upstanding Christian to be seen. The bigger problem, according to Pops and others, was that Sterling Jones had made it a "whites only" club Tuesday through Saturday. Negro folks got Sundays and Mondays. Melvin was very aware he was there on a Friday.

They hung their coats and dropped their cases in a vestibule, then entered the kitchen. Everyone turned at once and shouted greetings at Lenny.

"There he is!"

"Hey, Sax Man!"

There were eight staff, all Negroes, except for one woman who had the same coarse, wavy-curly black hair, dark eyebrows, and flashing eyes as Lenny.

A hulking man in a white cap called out, "Where you been, boy?" His forehead was glistening. His knife never stopped moving the whole time he spoke. "Grab your apron and get in here! Expecting a big crowd tonight. Cab Calloway big."

"Sorry, Sulli. Ma cut me loose."

"It's true," the woman who Melvin assumed was Lenny's mom said. "I'm giving him the night off, since he has a friend visiting." She smiled at Melvin. "Plus, it's Rosh Hashanah. Happy New Year, everyone!"

New year? What did she mean? It was September, not January.

"Hey, can we get the night off too?" one of the men called out, smiling. Others laughed.

"So, you are suddenly Jewish?" Mrs. Carini winked at Lenny from where she stood, her hands working a big ball of dough. "What I *won't* let my son get out of is giving his ma a big kiss. Come here, bubbie. And also, introduce your friend properly."

Lenny went to his mom, who was a little shorter than him, and planted one on her cheek. "Everyone, this is my friend, Melvin. Melvin, this is everyone." Lenny swept his arm through the air to indicate the whole staff. Melvin raised his hand in greeting.

"How 'bout your new buddy Melvin picks up a knife and earns that plate of food I can already see him fantasizin' about." People laughed. Was the man serious? Melvin didn't have the first idea how to handle a knife, especially not the way Sulli did. He hadn't slowed his lightning-fast chop since they'd entered the kitchen.

"Hello, Melvin." It was Mrs. Freeman from church. Melvin hadn't known she worked at the Harlem Club.

"Hhhhhello, MMMMrs. Ffffreeman."

Mrs. Carini wiped her hands on a towel and handed Lenny and Melvin each a paper cup filled with apple slices. Something like gold syrup had been poured over them. "It's a pleasure to meet you, Melvin. Welcome to our home."

Melvin nodded in appreciation. He took the cup and looked to Lenny for explanation.

"It's for Rosh Hashanah, the New Year. We don't celebrate it all out or Ma wouldn't be working tonight . . ."

"It's true," Mrs. Carini said. "I do my best, but I'm afraid I'm not raising you as orthodox as your father would have wanted me to."

"It's okay, Ma. I didn't mind missing the three-hour service, and we're still getting one of the best parts—the apples and honey."

Mrs. Carini swatted at her son. "Never mind him, Melvin. We usually go. It's a beautiful service. After, we throw pieces of bread into the Spokane River to represent letting go of our hurts and the ways we have hurt others. A good way to start the New Year."

Here was another group of people who gathered at the river, like the Spokane Indians once had.

"Please, eat," Mrs. Carini said, nodding at the cup in his hand.

Melvin pulled out one of the apple slices and quickly put it in his mouth before the honey dripped off. The golden sweetness spread across his tongue. He grinned.

"L'shanah tovah u'metukah," Mrs. Carini said, smiling warmly. "For a good and sweet year. Now, yalla, yalla, mishpachah!" she shouted suddenly. "We're down to the final hour."

"Wwwwhat was your mmmmom saying?" Melvin whispered. "Yalla?"

"It means 'to hurry.' *Mishpachah* means 'the family.' Like I said, they've been looking out for me since I was sitting in a playpen in the corner. Oh, hey, Ma?" Lenny threw his empty cup in a trash can. "The 'Dine-DANCE' sign is acting up again. Sparking and everything."

"Oy," she moaned.

Sulli spoke again. "I've been telling the boss he needs to get that fixed." He chopped with even more force. "Gonna lose more money on fines than it would cost just to replace the dang thing. Fire marshal already came by once."

"I know, I know," Mrs. Carini said. "Thank you, bubbie. I will make sure Mr. Jones knows. Now go on and have fun with your friend."

"See you later, Ma," Lenny said. He beckoned to Melvin to follow. "Come on, let's go meet the band!"

Already? Melvin's heart thumped harder. He hadn't been prepared to meet them straightaway.

They walked down a hallway barren enough to be in a hospital. The music coming through the double doors at the end wasn't like anything you'd *hear* in a hospital, although it sure sounded like it could be a magical cure for whatever might be ailing a person. Energetic and full of life.

Lenny's body vibrated like a lightbulb filament; his eyes were lit with excitement. "You ready for this?"

Melvin felt like a whole bunch of people were dancing the jitterbug in his stomach. No, he wasn't ready. Lenny forged ahead and Melvin followed in his wake.

Pushing through the swinging doors was like plunging into Curlew Lake, except they had jumped into a body of *sound* instead of water. Ten men in three rows blew brass—trumpets in the back, trombones in the middle, and saxes in the front. An armada of gold horns and brown faces wailed like coyotes at the moon. Under the wailing was a swinging-yet-steady, driving beat. The drummer, bassist, and pianist wove their strands into a braided belt that surrounded the brassy notes and held everything tight, including Melvin.

He bopped his head in time to the music. He had just started to hope it would go on forever when the musicians pulled the horns from their lips. The rhythm section also stopped playing, and it was silent. For about one second.

"Buick, man, you rushing it again," the drummer said to the bassist.

"No, dude, you're dragging," the bassist retorted.

One of the saxophonists up front spoke to a trombone player with the funny name of Idaho, and then directed the trombones to play their part again.

Lenny leaned in and whispered, "That's Gene, the bandleader."

When the trombones played alone, the sound wasn't nearly as impressive. More like a hand-pumped dolly instead of a train coming down the track.

Melvin stood against the wall and took in his surroundings. Black chairs with curved backs surrounded rows of rectangular tables covered in white tablecloths and decorated with candles in red glass holders. Central to everything was the wooden dance floor, shiny as Mr. Sterling Jones's bald head, which Melvin had seen pictured in club ads. The smell of the place was complex: polish, pomade, smoke, bleach, grease. Lots of grease. The perfumes and sweat and soap of all those folks had accumulated in the upholstery over twenty-plus years.

It struck him that even though actual people didn't mingle across the races here, their smells did—and also, that all the performers were Negro. Kitchen crew too, with the exception of Mrs. Carini. He glanced around, wondering when the white folks would start showing up, and how soon he would need to make himself scarce.

Gene the Bandleader counted off and they started up, the whole train roaring down the track again. A woman who'd been sitting on a stool, microphone in hand, stood. Though she wasn't particularly tall, her presence was magnific. And so was her voice. "It don't mean a thing, if it ain't got that swing. Doo-ah, doo-ah, doo-ah . . ." She sang about the rhythm being sweet or hot and it not mattering so long as you gave it everything you got, which clearly they were doing, even without a crowd.

They finished and Gene shaded his eyes with his hand, looking toward where Melvin and Lenny stood. "What you think, Sax Man? We ready for tonight?"

"You were born ready!" Lenny pulled Melvin toward the stage. Melvin's heart beat like the bass drum, reverberating up the back of his throat. *Boom. Boom. Ba-boom.*

"Who's your friend, Lenny?" the woman asked. She dabbed her face with a handkerchief.

"Miss Inez, guys, meet Mel Robinson."

Mel? Since when did Lenny call him Mel? Since right then, he supposed. At least it wasn't "Little Mel," like Uncle T called him.

One of the trumpeters called out, "Hey, Mel, do tell. Give us a yell. Was the music swell?"

Melvin's mouth was stuck.

"You done put the boy on the spot," Gene said. "Never mind that rhyming fool. Al's always fishing for compliments." He cast Al a sideways look. "And he talks bigger than King Kong."

Al responded with an impressive trill.

"Done showing off?" Gene asked before reaching out a hand to Melvin. "How you doing? I'm Gene."

Come on, mouth, cooperate. Melvin would have to shout to get his tongue over the initial block. "Yyyyou all are *a-muh-mazing!*" Not too bad.

Gene tipped his head in appreciation. "We've been playing together for a little while now."

"Mel plays accordion," Lenny announced.

Melvin's head snapped so fast in Lenny's direction it was a wonder he didn't break his neck. He waited for the hoots, hollers, and jeers.

"Well, all *right*, then!" Gene said. Others nodded and hummed their approval.

Melvin let out his breath and faced the band again. They hadn't mocked him, but what if they wanted to hear him play? The jitterbug started up in his stomach again.

"I once heard a brother do an accordion solo at a club in Seattle," Buick the Bassist said. "He tore it up! It was like he was playing piano, organ, and bass all at the same time. It was practically a religious experience."

It was hard to imagine. The one accordion performance Melvin had seen to date (other than that of his teacher, Mr. Javanovich) was on the *Lawrence Welk Show* when Mom called him in to watch two old white guys playing a waltz. The only religious experience it made him think of was a funeral. His own—if other boys found out he played. Gary and Troy flashed through his mind.

Melvin pulled on Lenny's arm. "Shhhh-ouldn't wwwe luh-let them puh-practice?" he muttered. He'd done okay when he'd spoken to the band. If he and Lenny left right then, the Thirteen Black Cats wouldn't have to know about the Stutter.

"They play these songs every night. They're not really practicing. They just love the music."

Gene had turned back to the band and was giving instructions for the next piece.

"Don't forget, Mr. Gene, I'm ready to blow with you whenever you want! I've been practicing every day."

Gene looked over his shoulder and smiled. "You keep at it, Sax Man, and you'll get your chance." He winked.

"Why not now?" Buick called. "These black cats *need* a little milk!"

The drummer punctuated the joke with a *ba-dump-bump* on his drum. Lenny looked at Gene expectantly, but the bandleader shook his head. "Not tonight, son, but soon."

Melvin felt Lenny deflate beside him. The band started up again. Within moments, Lenny's expression bounced back to its usual grin. "Come on. I gotta show you something!"

CHAPTER TEN

Melvin and Lenny rushed through the kitchen.

"Watch yourselves!" Mrs. Freeman called as she spun out of their way holding a large pan of cooked green beans.

"Grab your case!" Lenny shouted as they passed through the vestibule where their coats hung. He made a sharp turn into a stairwell and they scaled the steps. At the top, Lenny opened a door to his left. Melvin followed him into an apartment the size of a giant's shoebox.

"Do you want the mini tour or the deluxe?"

Melvin shrugged.

"Just kidding. There's not much to see, and we need to get to our jam session." He pointed to a table for two pushed up against the wall to their left. A bowl of lemons and a vase with daisies sat on top of the plastic tablecloth. "The dining room. Of course, we don't need a kitchen. Mom brings me dinner every night from the club and I go downstairs to have breakfast."

Restaurant food twice a day. *Yowza.* What he wouldn't give. Mom was an all right cook, but from the smells alone . . . Eating every day at the Harlem Club would be feasting like a king.

Lenny pointed to the couch against the right wall, past a hall entrance. "Ma's bedroom . . . a.k.a. the living room." A coffee table stood on a rag rug in front of the couch. He pointed to the window at the far end of the room. "Window." He grinned.

It was small and spare, but it wasn't sad. It was their home. Melvin walked to the window and looked out. An outdoor seating area—picnic tables in the midst of some scrubby pine trees— was down below. To the left of the window was a cabinet with glass doors and shelves that held dishes, vases, and, right in the center . . . a silver goblet. It wouldn't necessarily have stood out to Melvin, except that it reminded him of the photo he'd seen in Grandma's basement. Pops's friend had been holding a cup kind of like this one.

Next to it stood a framed picture of a man in uniform with a younger Mrs. Carini. The woman in the kitchen was a little plumper and had some gray hairs amidst the black, but it was definitely her. Melvin exhaled into his question: "Hhhis thuh-that your . . . your dad?" he asked. The man had a full face, slicked-back dark hair, and a grin as wide as Lenny's.

"Yep." Lenny had joined him at the cabinet.

"Wwwhat's that cuh-cup?"

"Oh, that's my dad's kiddush cup from when he became bar mitzvah. Sorry—you probably don't know . . . Jews say when you turn thirteen you become a man, responsible for your own choices and all that. The ceremony where it becomes official is called a bar mitzvah."

Shoot. When Melvin had turned thirteen, they'd had some cake and punch and he'd gotten a new baseball glove. Nothing that serious. He thought of the picture again. Had the boy been holding one of these kiddush cups? Had Pops had a Jewish friend too?

Lenny walked to another door just inside the entrance. He opened it and bowed deeply with a wave of his hand. "In case you have need . . ."

Melvin came over and peered inside. He had assumed the door led to a coat closet, but it was the toilet! A lightbulb hung from the ceiling. A small sink jutted from the wall. It was such tight quarters a person with a large backside might have trouble turning around to do his business.

"If you're wondering if I ever take a bath, there's a bigger shared bathroom down the hall." He closed the door.

Melvin would never complain about the size of their house or about having to share a room with Chuck ever again. Okay, maybe about being stuck with Chuck, but never the size of their home.

They walked the short hall to Lenny's room. The first thing Melvin saw was the New York Giants' Willie Mays. He made a beeline for the poster over Lenny's bed and touched the signature.

"My grandpa sent it to me after Willie got named Most Valuable Player last year. My grandpa's a die-hard Giants fan. Lived in New York his whole life. I've never been there myself, but I'll be there one day—playing at Birdland."

"Buh-buh-buh-birds?" Melvin jerked his head. "Hhh-that would be a nuh-noisy audience."

"Ha-ha. Keep working on your material." Lenny went to the phonograph sitting on a stand near the end of his bed and pulled out an LP from the cabinet below. "You don't know Birdland?"

Melvin shook his head.

"Whenever the walls of this place start to close in on me, I put this disc on and I'm in New York, sitting front and center." He handed the album cover to Melvin. *Charlie Parker Quintet with Fats Navarro and Bud Powell, Live at Birdland, May 17, 1950.*

The sound was *crazy.* Notes jumping all over the place as if there were hot coals under their feet. Melvin liked it.

About halfway through the A side, Lenny pulled out his sax. He knew the part perfectly. When the tune ended, Melvin applauded heartily. "Hhhhow long did it take to mmm—"

"Memorize all that?" Lenny looked at the ceiling; he was thinking. "About a year, I guess. I've played it at least once a day since I got the album. One day, I hope to be as good as the guys on the record." He motioned with his chin. "Get out your squeeze-box, man. Let's play!"

Keeping up with the hot-coal-walking notes would be like Tuck the turtle trying to keep up with Jesse Owens, the Olympic track star. And he was horrible at improv. "I'm nuh-not—" He tapped quickly. "Guh-good enough for that."

"That's all right. I've got something else for us anyway. This is what I wanted to show you." Lenny pulled a piece of sheet music out of a drawer in his desk. The title was written across the top in Lenny's chicken-scratch handwriting: "It Don't Mean a Thing (If It Ain't Got That Swing)." "You know this one, right? It's older, but it's a classic. The band was playing it downstairs."

Melvin nodded. "Duh-don't know hhhhow to puh-play it, though."

"Look, I wrote the chords across the top. All you got to do is play that for now. Forget the melody." Lenny sure liked to work that grin of his.

Melvin could read music, so he knew exactly where Lenny was. He expanded and contracted his accordion, pushing the buttons for the chords. It actually didn't sound too bad, since Lenny carried the melody. Melvin hit a wrong chord once or twice, but he caught his mistakes the moment the notes were in the air.

When they finished, Lenny slapped him on the back. "That was boss, man!"

Melvin shrugged. They weren't going to be appearing on stages together anytime soon.

"Hey, you know the show *Starlit Stairway*?" Lenny asked.

Of course, he did. Everyone in Spokane, especially those with televisions, knew *Starlit Stairway*. It was a variety show that showcased local kids' talents. The twins who sang the jingle at the beginning were more famous around town than Grace Kelly.

"So, I've been thinking: *Starlit Stairway*, you and me, playing this tune. What do you say?"

You've been smelling too much formaldehyde in science class, is what Melvin wanted to say. But his tongue was in a vise and it was easier just to shake his head. He waved his hands in front of his chest to make sure Lenny got the message. No way.

"What? Why not? We already sound pretty good. Imagine what we'd sound like after practicing for a month?"

"You don't nuh-nuh-need . . . Go on there *yourself*."

"That would be boring, man. Music needs layers."

He talked as if music were a lasagna.

"It needs *texture*."

Or some kind of fabric.

"I need you to lay down a bass line for me. I need some higher notes up top. I need some chords to make it richer, more satisfying."

Now he sounded like an advertisement for chocolate cake. "You ssssound like you're tuh-talking about food."

"I am. Food for the *soul*." He grinned so big Melvin thought his face might split. "So, are you in, or are you in?"

Melvin shook his head again, but Lenny was like a broken television set. He wasn't receiving the signal. "Great! We'll be famous, man!"

Lenny might be famous. Melvin would be laughed out of school. He played the *accordion*! Oh, and he stuttered. Which he was not about to do on public television for the whole Inland Empire to witness.

"Now all we need to do is come up with our stage names."

Melvin had a stage name for his friend already: Lenny "Crazy Man" Carini. Because if Lenny thought he was going to play accordion—and risk stuttering—in front of thousands of TV viewers, he was off his rocker.

CHAPTER ELEVEN

The next morning, the newspaper's sports section headline read, "Cleveland High Tigers Claw Their Way Back." Chuck had led the football team to its first win of the season with three touchdowns (after the previous week's blowout, which he'd been forced to watch from the sidelines). The sportswriter had dubbed him Spokane's "Reigning Running Back" and given him the nickname "Touchdown Titan."

At breakfast, Chuck announced his nickname for himself—"End Zone Emperor"—which got him lots of razzing from the rest of the Robinsons before he and Pops walked out the door, headed for the golf course. Chuck went along as Pops's caddy—carrying clubs and keeping score—although he'd told Melvin it was about time for him to take over the job.

Thankfully, Melvin didn't have to start that morning. He lay in his bed after they left, reading *20,000 Leagues Under the Sea* for English class. He related to the sailors in the story, who hunt a mysterious sea creature and get taken captive in a submarine. He had his own personal sea monster—his tongue—trying to take him down.

* * *

A while later, he and Maisy sat at the table diligently doing homework, while in their parents' bedroom Mom and Marian conferred about her Homecoming gown.

Melvin broke the silence. "Hey, you remember that puh-picture of PPPPops with that buh-boy?"

Maisy looked up from her spelling primer. "With the fancy silver cup?"

He nodded. "Wwwould you get it for me the next time you go?"

"What about you?"

He was content with his buck-fifty for a job half-done. "Jjjjjust guh-get it for me, will you?"

"Sure. I bet Granny will give me the other half of your money too. I'm going to put it toward my new typewriter!"

Marian and Mom came through the kitchen doorway, talking about which flowers would look best with cream-colored satin. Mom took a seat behind her sewing machine in the kitchen nook. She'd been working all morning on a wedding dress for the Buchners' daughter. Mr. Buchner was a bigwig at the aluminum plant. Melvin had heard Pops and his buddies say there weren't any jobs for Negroes at the plant other than custodian or, if they really liked a man and he was willing to work twice as hard and get paid half as much, a line worker.

"May I go to Darlene's now to study?" Marian asked.

"That sounds fine," Mom said. "But be back by two and we'll measure you for your gown." Mom's voice rose with excitement. "I'll be starting it the *moment* I finish this." She lifted the wedding dress.

"Thank you, Mama," Marian said, kissing her cheek. "That's beautiful, by the way."

"Yours will be even more beautiful," Mom said, "because you'll be the one wearing it."

Marian smiled graciously and left through the back door.

A while later, they heard footsteps on the front porch. At the sound of the mailbox door shutting, Maisy jumped up and ran out of the room.

"Margaret Ruth Robinson, slow down already! You almost stepped on this expensive tulle with your carelessness!" The fluffy, white fabric billowed from the nook like bubbles overflowing a tub.

"Sorry, Mama!" she called from the living room.

"What are we going to do with that girl?" Mom muttered. "Reckless. Going to catch up to her one of these days."

"Don't look at mmmme," Melvin said, looking up from his math book. "She's your child."

"We are each of us our brother's keeper," Mom intoned.

"She's not mmmy buh-buh-buh-*brother*, *is* she?" He grinned. That was funny, even if Mom wouldn't agree.

"And *you*. That smart mouth of yours is going to catch up to you too."

Stubborn mouth was more like it. He wanted to be as smooth as Sammy Davis, Jr., and not just when he sang. Pops thought Sammy was too slick for his own good. Thought the performer didn't want to be associated with his own people. But who was Pops to judge? Like Uncle T had pointed out, they had moved into this neighborhood with mostly white people instead of getting a house on the east side.

Mom kept glancing his way. When she cleared her throat for the third time, he knew she had something to say and was trying to figure out how.

"So, is everything going all right at Cleveland for you?"

He shrugged. "S'okay, I ssss'pose."

"You'll let us know if you're having any troubles at all, won't you?"

He nodded, even though he didn't see how that would help. His parents couldn't sit in class and speak for him.

"I'm glad you made this new friend. Lenny? If you want to invite him over here, you're welcome to."

He lifted his chin in acknowledgment.

"And Melvin, I want you to know I pray every day for you. Got the ladies' auxiliary at church praying too. God's going to heal you. I just know it."

Melvin squinted at his mother, whose eyes were fixed on the pearls she was hand-sewing onto the dress. He blinked. If God planned to heal him, why give him this broken tongue in the first place?

"Go check on your sister, please. She's been out there longer than it takes to retrieve mail from her own front porch. And I don't want her getting distracted from her homework. Probably out there reading this week's *Jet*."

Another of Maisy's aspirations was to write for *Jet*, a Negro publication that covered news about their community and the events that mattered to them.

He found her sitting on the top step, the magazine already flipped open in her lap. The mailbox door gaped as if it'd seen something shocking at the house across the street. He went to shut it and found mail still inside.

"Melvin, look." Her voice sounded small. She pointed to a photo.

It was upside down from Melvin's perspective, so he sat next to her. He read the headline: "Nation Horrified by Murder of Kidnaped Chicago Youth."

Beneath the title was a photo of a boy and his mom. The mom was smiling at someone off to the side, but the boy gazed straight at the camera. Melvin made two quick assessments about the boy: he looked confident, and he was around Melvin's age.

Maisy turned the page and let out a small cry.

The gruesomeness of what Melvin saw made him want to look away and at the same time held his eyes captive. The mom, who had been smiling just a page before, now stood before a dead body in a suit. A closeup showed what should have been the dead person's head, but the face was so disfigured it looked like the innards of a deer Pops had bagged while hunting. Or like a pile of rocky, lumpy dirt. Melvin stared at the picture, trying to make sense of it. It was like one of Pops's jigsaw puzzles, but where the face should have been, someone had put the wrong piece. He just couldn't make the connection to the confident, smiling boy in the first picture.

Melvin took the magazine from Maisy's hands and scanned the article. A white woman had accused the boy, Emmett Till, of being inappropriate. He had been visiting family in the South, but he himself was from Chicago.

"He was killed in Mississippi," Maisy whispered, as if afraid to wake a ghost. "Where Shyla is from." Maisy and Shyla, Mrs. Matilda

Jenkins's niece, had hit it off at the Jessups' cookout and become pen pals. They had exchanged a couple letters already.

Melvin gripped the edges of the magazine. The juniper bushes on either side of the steps gave off their pungent odor in the heat, like incense rising to heaven. Melvin felt woozy. He feared if he kept staring at the pictures he might tumble into the scene and be there with the sad mom and the dead, beaten boy.

Maisy jumped up, yanking the magazine from his hands. "Mama! Mama!" She ran into the house. Melvin followed, slowly, dumbly, as heavy as an elephant moving through molasses. When he got inside, Maisy had her arms wrapped around Mom's middle, like an octopus clinging to a pylon. Mom stared at the photo. The wedding dress was on the floor.

"Sweet Jesus in heaven," Mom gasped. She clutched the open magazine to her chest as if trying to comfort the boy and his mother. "Why in God's name would they ever print such a horrific thing?" She sounded outraged, but in her eyes Melvin saw fear. She grabbed Melvin by the arm and pulled him in tight.

Why in God's name would anyone ever *do* such a horrific thing? was what he wanted to know.

CHAPTER TWELVE

Monday—September 19, he would never forget it—Melvin resolved to bring up Emmett Till's death in Mrs. Stimson's class. It was social studies, after all, the "study of human society," as she had called it on the first day. And he wanted to know what in human society would make it possible for humans—*grown men*—to commit such a grisly, inhumane act against another human—a boy only a little older than himself, Melvin had confirmed when rereading the *Jet* article.

He walked to school a few paces behind Chuck, Marian, and Darlene. Marian and Darlene complained about a girl, formerly a friend, who also had been nominated for Homecoming Queen and was now "putting on airs" around them.

Melvin could not care less about that. The image of Emmett Till's battered face had been seared into his memory. His family had talked about the murder around the dinner table the night before. Chuck seemed unaffected. "Mississippi is practically another country," he'd scoffed.

Marian agreed. "That would never happen here. We know a lot of white people and they treat us just fine."

"That may be true," Pops said, breaking his silence. "But so long as Negroes anywhere are maligned and trampled upon, none of us can rest easy. And while you might not realize it, white people have put up walls here too, trying to keep us out of certain places."

Maisy had been incensed. "This is why I'm going to be a reporter—to make sure people around the world hear about these things. People need to know the truth!"

Melvin had agreed most with Maisy, although he hadn't said anything during the conversation, and he didn't have any desire to be a reporter.

Once he got to school, he dropped the books he didn't need in his locker. He didn't see Lenny so he headed for homeroom.

Gary, Troy, a boy named Larry Schmidt, and another boy Melvin didn't recognize walked toward him. Gary was an atomic bomb with detection radar, and it was clear Melvin was his target. Melvin put his head down and planned to blow by them. His anxiety mounted with each step; his breathing got shallower. Suddenly, he was hemmed in on all sides, his back to the row of lockers, his breath trapped in his lungs.

"How's it going, Skip?" Gary smelled like gasoline. "Wanted to introduce you to our new friend, Johnny."

Johnny, whose short black hair stood on end like the bristles of a brush, shoved his hands in his trouser pockets and lifted his skinny chin in greeting.

"He just moved into town," Gary went on, "and Principal Brill asked me to show him around. Make sure he knows where everything is. Johnny, this is the local idiot."

Johnny's small eyes registered a flash of concern. His lips twitched as if he wasn't sure whether to smile or frown.

Melvin gripped his book as if it were a brick, and imagined himself knocking Gary's block off with it. His whole body was rigid—perfect conditions for the Stutter to have free rein.

Troy spoke, probably wanting to make sure Johnny saw him as a leader of the pack too. "Go on." He nudged Melvin. "Be polite. Introduce yourself."

"Yeah," Gary said, "you don't want to be rude to the new kid, do you?"

Johnny's expression had changed at least three times during the encounter, from what looked like confusion to embarrassment and then to awareness that he was being let in on a really great joke by these boys whose opinion could make a huge difference for his time at Cleveland High. Lucky him.

Melvin's eyes darted around the circle, and then to the end of the hall, willing Lenny to appear. Everything was a blur of dresses and coats and white skin.

He scratched his head, trying to jump-start his mouth.

"What's the matter with him?" Johnny asked.

"Nnnnn . . ." He pushed the sound up and out, but his lips were locked tight and refused to open. Nothing! he wanted to shout, but of course, that wasn't true. Clearly, something *was* wrong with him. The gravelly buzzing that came from his throat sounded imbecilic. Deranged and dangerous, even to himself.

"See? What'd we tell you? He's a dimwit!"

Johnny glanced around nervously, looking everywhere but at Melvin. Then he gave a little smile, and then a laugh, and then they were elbowing each other and gesturing toward Melvin, as if to say,

Your turn! Isn't it fun? You can get the weirdo to make a funny-strange sound!

Melvin watched as Gary's and Troy's cruelty spread to Johnny until he was all-the-way infected. Johnny laughed and laughed with them while Melvin struggled to get control of his voice and let them know he was *not* a joke.

That's when he saw Chuck. His brother was in the center of a group of other juniors coming down the hall, talking and laughing. He tossed and caught his football as he walked. He glanced Melvin's way.

Their eyes met.

He dropped the ball and went after it, but he had seen Melvin. No doubt about it. He had seen him suffocating under the weight of his words, trapped by these boys who he *knew* were mean and punishing when it came to Melvin's trouble with speaking.

Chuck glanced back once as his friends forged ahead. He and Melvin locked eyes again.

Help me!

Chuck shook his head and kept walking.

The movement was so slight, Melvin hoped for a moment that he'd imagined it. But he knew better. Chuck was not going to save him.

First bell rang—the warning that they had minutes to get to class—and Melvin charged forward, busting through the hedge the other boys had made around him. He stalked to homeroom, bile burning in his throat.

In class, Millie gave him a small smile as he walked toward his seat. He lifted his hand to say hello, his stomach roiling. No way around it—if he spoke up in class, he would stutter, he was so worked up from the encounter in the hall. Gary and Troy entered the room, seemingly without a care in the world. Johnny, still with them, greeted Mrs. Stimson before finding an empty seat.

Lenny rushed in as the final bell rang. Their teacher raised a disapproving eyebrow at him.

Melvin felt a rush of anger toward Lenny. Of all the days to be late, why *that* day? He could have really used Lenny's help. They exchanged looks, but their teacher had begun roll call, and even if she hadn't, Melvin wouldn't have felt like talking to him anyway.

He *had* to say something about what he'd seen in *Jet*, however, and if Mrs. Stimson got started on her lesson for the day, he knew he would let it go. It was now or never. As soon as the Pledge was recited, he raised his hand. A drop of sweat trickled down his armpit.

"Melvin?" The note of surprise in Mrs. Stimson's voice was obvious. "You want to say something?"

He sure did. He wanted to say, A boy was killed. But he was afraid he'd snag on the B and get stuck there, the sound echoing in the dead-silent room.

So instead, he said, "Emmett Tuh-till."

Having a warm-up to the M seemed to help. Like having a stepladder to make the leap over the fence more doable.

Mrs. Stimson glanced around the room, gauging the class's response to the boy's name. "Yes. A very . . . unfortunate incident." She shifted her focus to the blackboard as if planning to move on.

"He was kuh-kuh-kuh—" Melvin jerked his head, half voluntarily, but it also felt like a spasm, out of his control. He was grateful no one laughed, although he guessed the Rat was smirking behind his back.

"KILLED!" he shouted. It was the only way to expel the word from his mouth.

Kids murmured around the room.

"What's he talking about?" someone whispered.

"Who was killed?" someone else asked.

"Now, Melvin, there's no need to shout. I will have to ask you to leave the room if you get yourself, or others"—she glanced around—"worked up over this."

Lenny raised his hand, but Melvin spoke before Mrs. Stimson could call on him. This was his to do, *his* to bring up.

"Did you see the puh-puh—" The sea monster was pulling him under. "PICTURE?" he shouted.

More murmuring, some titters.

"No, I did not. You yelled again, Melvin. This is your last warning."

Melvin fumed. How could he get across to her that he wasn't trying to be disrespectful? It was the only way to say what he needed to say. *What needed to be said.*

Lenny's hand remained in the air.

"Yes, Lenny," Mrs. Stimson said.

"Mrs. Stimson, I for one would like to hear what Melvin has to say. It must be important if . . ."

He trailed off, but Melvin could fill in the rest. If Melvin is willing to speak about it in front of the class.

"I'm sorry, Lenny, Melvin, but I have a prepared lesson. I must insist that you drop this subject. It's not appropriate for school, and anyway, that happened in the South, where they have those kinds of problems. Besides, it sounded like the boy had less than impeccable manners. A reminder for you all." She turned and wrote on the board: C-O-L-D.

Cold. That was her response, all right.

W-A-R, she finished, explaining the essay they would be writing on whether the Cold War was an actual war, with support for their argument, of course.

Melvin could see out of the corner of his eye that Lenny was trying to get his attention, but he kept his gaze fixed straight ahead.

So it was *appropriate* to talk about the atomic bombs that killed a hundred thousand Japanese and it was *appropriate* to talk about the annihilation of Jews in World War II, but they couldn't talk about the murder of one teenaged boy in the United States of America?

He was our age! Melvin wanted to shout. He was a kid, just like us!

Except, Melvin thought, sinking lower in his seat, he wasn't "just like" the vast majority of the kids in his class or at Cleveland High, or in the entire city of Spokane, for that matter. At least not from their perspective.

He was a Negro boy.

CHAPTER THIRTEEN

hen Melvin came into homeroom on Thursday, a film projector was set up. His apprehension turned to excitement as he slipped into his chair. He loved movies. Especially classroom movies. When a movie was showing, no one was talking.

Lenny was already there. "Hey, did your mom tell you I called yesterday?"

"Yeah. I don't . . ."

Gary and Troy appeared.

Melvin stared at his folded hands on his desk. He'd been about to tell Lenny he didn't talk on the phone, but just the sight of those boys caused lockjaw to set in.

"All right!" Nick Graves said when he saw the projector. "Do we get popcorn too?"

Several kids, many of whom were huddled in small groups, laughed at the joke. Millie sat alone, as usual, seemingly unaffected by the jostling and twittering going on around her. She carried around a heaviness, Melvin thought. It emanated like a solemn perfume.

"Settle down, everyone, and take your seats." Mrs. Stimson didn't sound like she was in a joking mood. Then again, she never did.

Roll call was no longer a big deal. Mrs. Stimson automatically looked up when she got to Melvin's name so that he never had to answer. During the Pledge, he still tried to make it look as though he were reciting, when really he was just mouthing the words. It felt ridiculous, flapping his lips around like that, but at least no one seemed to notice.

That morning, however, Gary leaned in from behind. "I can't hear you, Skip. You really should speak up when you're pledging allegiance to our great nation."

Mrs. Stimson peered at Gary, hand on her heart, waiting for him to notice her teacher's glare. Melvin remained tense, like a deer in a hunter's presence.

As they took their seats, Mrs. Stimson released her eye-hold on Gary. Her gaze turned to the class more generally. "Our country is currently engaged in a war. True or false?" She wanted them to defend their Cold War essays.

Chaz Burlington raised his hand. "I say no. A war has casualties. The Cold War is just about countries trying to look big and powerful."

Sounds familiar, Melvin thought, imagining Gary and Troy flexing their muscles in the seats behind him. He had read in *Popular Science* about how the U.S. and Russia were in a race to build nuclear weapons as a way of flexing their metaphoric muscles. Not only had the U.S. been the first to use atomic weapons in battle—decimating the populations of two Japanese cities—they had tested an even more powerful one in the Pacific Ocean not that long ago. An entire *island*, unpopulated this time, had been vaporized in an instant. Now you see it, now you don't.

Millie raised her hand. Millie was going to speak? She hadn't volunteered a comment yet. "The Korean War had casualties, and it was a result of the United States feeling the need to stop the growth of Communism around the world, which is at the heart of the Cold War. So, the Cold War *has* had casualties. *Many.*"

Mrs. Stimson crossed her arms. "Let's talk more about the relationship between the United States and Russia, a country ruled by Communism, which Millie mentioned. Communism is the opposite of freedom, but there are some Americans who haven't liked our stance against Russia and have spoken out. Public figures, such as Paul Robeson."

Katie Sugarman raised her hand. "Who's that?"

Mrs. Stimson glanced at Baron Carter and then at Melvin. Oh no. Melvin knew who Paul Robeson was, all right, but only because Marian fancied herself a future opera star, and not because he was a Negro like Mr. Robeson, as he had a feeling Mrs. Stimson was thinking.

"Perhaps Baron or Melvin could tell us?"

Baron just shrugged. Melvin looked straight ahead, not confirming or denying the answer to her question.

"He's a boss opera singer who was also an actor and professional football player," Lenny interjected, without raising his hand.

Melvin looked at him, impressed. Apparently, his knowledge of Negro musicians went beyond jazz.

"A football player who sings opera? That's a first," Nick said.

"He must not have been very good. I've never heard of him," Gary said.

"Lenny is correct, in spite of speaking out of turn." Mrs. Stimson paused, letting the correction sink in. "Indeed, Mr. Robeson is multi-talented. A credit to his race. However, any hope of continuing his career ended when he set himself against the United States by saying no Negro would fight in a war against Russia."

Melvin didn't blame Mr. Robeson. As Grandma Robinson was fond of saying, "No one wins in a war." War was like Exhibit A in the case for human insanity. A mirror showing humans how good they were at destroying themselves. Personally, Melvin never wanted to have anything to do with it.

"But we don't really have a choice," Mrs. Stimson said, as if responding to his thoughts. "We must fight back or Communism will spread and dominate our world." It was hard not to imagine their teacher standing in a TV studio kitchen, except instead of advertising refrigerators, she was promoting democracy.

"How many of you know that from February to May of this year, our government tested atomic bombs right here on American soil?"

Melvin hadn't known *that*.

"You mean, like blew them up?" Troy asked.

"That's right. In the state of Nevada."

"*Whoa*." Troy and Gary said in tandem.

"Operation Cue took place on May fifth. The government built several houses and then detonated an atomic bomb to see which houses would provide the best shelter. Six thousand people were there to watch."

"Oh man," Gary said. "I would have loved to see that."

"Thanks to the cameras they placed throughout what they called 'Survival Town,' we will get an even better view than the spectators." Mrs. Stimson moved to the back of the classroom. "Linda, will you turn out the lights, please?"

The room went dark except for the fluttering of light on the screen at the front. Kids whispered to each other excitedly, as if they were about to watch the latest episode of *Adventures of Superman* instead of a display of people's ability to end life on Earth.

The opening music sounded like it was from a superhero movie. This show was not presented by Kellogg's, though. This one had been brought to them by the Federal Civil Defense Administration. A man's deep voice told them about the bomb that would be exploded and about the structures that had been built.

A single-story house without a basement. A two-story house made of brick. A house made of eight-inch concrete block and reinforced steel. A box-type shelter in a basement. All these homes, created just to be destroyed.

Strangely, they didn't leave the houses empty. They populated them with "people"—mannequins dressed in everyday clothes, which they also wanted to test. For what, Melvin wasn't sure. How was some flimsy fabric supposed to stand up to a thirty-kiloton blast? Then the announcer told them that the mannequins represented "Mr. and Mrs. America."

They were all white people.

A lady mannequin stood stiffly in a living room. Father and son mannequins waited patiently in a basement shelter. Rows of stiff white Mr. and Mrs. Americas hung on poles facing the blast, like criminals waiting to be executed.

There were other structures too. Transformer substations. Power lines. Radio towers. They wanted to see how quickly electricity and communications could be reestablished after an attack. That actually sounded interesting. The rest of it was just plain creepy.

The movie cut to early morning, before the blast. Dozens of buses and cars made their way to the observation site in the pre-dawn darkness. Television cameras were set up on a hill to broadcast the test into the homes of all Americans. Civil Defense workers settled into their trenches relatively close to ground zero.

A man's voice droned over a loudspeaker. "H-minus one minute. If you don't have goggles, you must turn away from the blast. In H-minus ten seconds . . . nine . . . eight . . . seven . . ."

When the blast went off, the screen flashed white. The classroom momentarily filled with light. Millie, her profile outlined by the flash, had her eyes closed, as if in prayer.

Slowly, the spectators in their goggles reappeared. The searing light had made it momentarily impossible to see, like Saul on his way to Damascus when the Lord struck him down with a brilliance that left him groping for his donkey.

A huge, white mushroom cloud ripped through the sky. The movie cut to the single-story home. It appeared to be engulfed in heat waves. In less than a second, it was obliterated. The whole room gasped. Millie's eyes remained shut, but Melvin was certain she had flinched. The film showed one building after the next—completely blown away by the force. The whole time, Millie sat diagonal to the screen, her eyes like closed curtains.

The United States was the only country that had ever used these bombs to kill people.

Japanese people.

Melvin wondered suddenly, Did Millie have family there? Had any of them been affected?

The movie continued, showing the Civil Defense workers twenty-four hours later, pulling a broken mannequin from the rubble. The narrator made it clear that while basement shelters provided some degree of protection, they couldn't be depended on completely in potential blast situations.

No kidding, Melvin thought. Based on the stunned silence around the room, Melvin knew he wasn't the only one thinking this. He recalled Bert the Turtle from the comic book they'd been given the previous year to show them what to do in case of a bomb attack. Bert, like Tuck, pulled his head and legs into his shell. They were supposed to roll into a ball with their arms around their heads. How that would protect them from a bomb that vaporized whole buildings—whole islands, even? It was ludicrous. People were fooling themselves.

The final bizarre scene showed a mannequin on a pole. His suit coat had faded, but he was still intact. All the workers sat around outside, eating food from containers that had been present at the explosion. It dawned on Melvin that the purpose of this film might actually have been to make them all feel better about their chances of surviving an attack. He wasn't buying it.

The narrator concluded, "It must be borne in mind that multi-megaton weapons would result in much greater damage over a larger area. All these factors must be considered as we plan for survival for our homes, our families, and our nation in the nuclear age."

Plan for survival? What a joke. If the Soviets ever decided to drop a bomb on Fairchild Air Force Base, Spokane would be wiped from the face of the earth.

Sorry, Grandma Robinson, but a basement shelter wasn't going to cut it.

CHAPTER FOURTEEN

illie sat with her back to the rest of the cafeteria. Gloria Rayburn, from homeroom, sat next to her. Her blond ponytail bobbed as she spoke.

Melvin started to turn around, but Lenny waved him back in Millie's direction from across the room, an urgent look on his face. He never should have told Lenny his plan to seek her out. He gripped his lunch tray and approached slowly, hearing himself say over and over: "Hello, may I join you?"

He had learned to survive the lunch line by pointing at what he wanted . . . Maybe he could just point to the seat across from Millie. But then what? Would he just sit there like a "mutant," as Maisy had called him, while the two girls went on chatting?

His body lumbered forward, but his thoughts had him turning and going the other way as quickly as possible. The sensation was like riding in the passenger seat of a car going too fast, like the time he'd ridden shotgun with Uncle T, right after his uncle had gotten his brand-new Bel Air. There in the lunchroom, Melvin's body was in the driver's seat while his brain was screaming, Too fast! Brake!

He arrived at their table. The girls looked up at once—and Melvin's rehearsed line flew from his mind.

Millie's eyes took on a friendly look, but she didn't say anything. He stood there, afraid to open his mouth.

"I just remembered I needed to talk to Shirley about drill team," Gloria said, gathering her lunch and standing. "I'll see you later." She walked away.

Millie's thin eyebrows lifted. The dimples on either side of her smile appeared. She shrugged and gestured to the seat across from her, saying without words that he was free to join her.

Melvin sat and then picked up his fork, too nervous to look up. He expected her eyes to reflect a mixture of curiosity, tolerance, and most of all pity, which he really didn't want to see. When the silent tension had frayed to the breaking point, he glanced in her direction.

Kindness. That was all.

He could do this. With control, not tension. As Mr. Feuchtinger said, neither relaxation nor tension was the goal, but strength and flexibility. Stuttering was a matter of strengthening muscles and gaining greater control, especially for people whose thoughts moved more quickly than their mouths. *That's me, all right,* he had thought when he read it.

"Hhhello, Mmmm—"

It's simple, dummy. Millie!

He was plunged into a pool of shame. Why had he opened his mouth? *M*'s got him stuck faster than quicksand every time. And the silence had been perfectly fine. For both of them, it had seemed. His lips and tongue were solid ice; the rest of his face was hot enough to melt the North Pole.

"How are you, Melvin?" Her voice was warm water.

He smiled and his lips and tongue relaxed. "I-I wuh-wanted to mmmmake sure you wwwwere okay," he said.

The smooth skin between her brows wrinkled. "Okay?"

"The ffffilm? I wuh-wuh-wondered if it . . . upset you."

She considered him for a moment. "Did it upset you?"

"I . . ." He wasn't stuck on his words. He hadn't expected her to turn the question around on him. But since she *had* . . . "I ssssuppose it . . ." His forehead tensed. He nodded.

She looked down at her food—clumps of rice and what looked like canned meat held together with some kind of papery green wrapper.

He didn't know how to say what he wanted to next. He might as well be direct. "Duh-did your ffffamily know anyone who died? In Japan. Because of the . . ." *Bomb* would not come. "Explosion?" He watched her carefully.

"Honestly, I don't know. My parents have never spoken of it." She tilted her head and looked at him again.

He wanted to look away and he didn't. There was something in her eyes, or maybe in the line between her eyebrows . . . or maybe it was the way she held her mouth just so. What was going on in her thoughts?

Finally, she spoke. "They don't talk about anything related to the war." She looked down at the table. "I think it's too painful."

Melvin chewed his sandwich, pondering what she'd revealed. His parents didn't talk about where they came from either. Was it too painful for them as well? Or did parents just not talk about these things?

He swallowed and immediately bit off more. If he kept eating, maybe she would keep talking . . . and he wouldn't have to.

"I didn't want to see the buildings shatter," she went on. "In the film, I mean."

He nodded, hoping he looked as interested as he felt.

"I don't want it to seem normal. It's *not* normal."

He nodded some more. They were quiet again.

Then suddenly, "We were taken away. Forced from our home."

He felt confused. What was she talking about? The question must have shown on his face.

"After Japan attacked Pearl Harbor."

Melvin was very familiar with the bombing of Pearl Harbor, of course, from the stories about his uncle. But what did she mean they were taken away?

"Many Japanese families were put in these camps during the war. I was only one year old, but we were there for three years, and we couldn't leave."

He couldn't believe what he was hearing. Of course he believed *her*, he just couldn't believe . . .

He opened his mouth and tried to ease out the first sound, like Mr. Feuchtinger suggested. "Whhhoo?" He sounded a little like an owl, but it didn't matter. Keep going, he thought. "Ssssent you away?"

"The U.S. government." She said it without any judgment about his not having known. "President Roosevelt issued an executive order."

He felt his eyes widen. The government? The *democratic* federal government? That didn't sound very "democratic" to him. "Juh-just for buh-being Japanese?"

She nodded. "We were considered the enemy. My parents have never said anything. But my brother remembered a lot and he told me about it."

"Do you remember anything?" Melvin asked, completely swept up in what she was telling him.

"The soldiers. They had long guns with pointy knives on the ends. I remember being so scared of them. And the barbed wire on the fences. Sometimes I have nightmares."

He looked intently in her eyes. He had nightmares too. One in particular had shown up repeatedly over the past few months. In it, someone was spooning cement down his throat. It hardened in his mouth, causing him to choke.

She went on, "Usually, I'm lying in a dark room. There are moans and groans all around me. In one, a poisonous spider lands on me, but my arms are paralyzed and I can't get it off. I lie there as it walks all over my face. There's nothing I can do, except scream. Sometimes I wake up and wonder if I've screamed out loud." Her gaze dropped to her hands in her lap.

Melvin's heart raced. "Thhhh-at sounds awful," he said.

She remained quiet but gave him a small, appreciative smile.

"I ssstill huh-have it," he said.

Her eyebrows pulled together. She looked as if she was waiting for him to say more.

He dug into his pocket and pulled out the small turtle.

Her smile lit up her face, setting off fireworks in his chest. He noticed that her front teeth turned in just a little. It made her even more likable. She was real.

"I remember," she said.

He wanted to ask what made her put it on his desk that day, even though he didn't really need to. It was her kindness. Her seeing him—*really* seeing him—and caring.

"Here's something I think about a lot," she said. "I'm American, not Japanese. This is my home. It's the only home I've ever known. But sometimes . . ."

She started to wrap up her lunch. Did she plan to finish her sentence?

"Sssometimes wuh-what?"

She peered into his face, as if she were deciding again whether to say what was on her mind.

What was on *his* mind was, I really like you. But he said, "I really want to know." Not a single hitch.

"Sometimes . . ." She looked around the room, lowered her voice. "I think all these white kids don't have any idea what it feels like to be different. To be the only one, or one of very few. You know what I mean."

He nodded vehemently. Of course, he knew!

"I say the Pledge of Allegiance right along with them but I know they don't see me as a *real* American. They think *they* are the only real Americans."

Wow. He had no idea she felt this way.

"Do you ever have the feeling that you're just being allowed to rent space here? But if the landlord decides he doesn't like you anymore, you'll be out on the street?"

He'd never thought that, actually. He wasn't even sure what she meant. Clearly, she wasn't talking about a literal landlord. Did she mean in their neighborhood? In Spokane? In the United States?

"I said I'm not Japanese, but that's not exactly true, because that is the country my family came from—originally. Sometimes, I feel like a nonnative flower that's been transplanted. So I wonder, can I actually survive here?"

Melvin wanted to say he knew exactly what she meant, but that would be a lie. Once again, where was *here*?

Say something! he shouted at himself.

"It's nice talking to you," she said.

You too, he wanted to say, but his tongue was suddenly tight again.

"What I mean is, you're nice to talk to." She looked away shyly. "I've never felt like I could tell anyone those things. But I knew I could tell you."

His heart thrummed. She stood to go.

"You're very good at listening, Melvin." With that, she left.

Melvin felt himself beam. He had done it. He had talked to Millie Takazawa. So why did he still feel like he'd swallowed one of Chuck's weights?

Lenny was over in a flash, slapping Melvin on the back and asking a million questions, including had he asked her to the Homecoming Dance?

Melvin brushed off the suggestion, but thought, Maybe I could get up the nerve—after today. Then he remembered Mr. Takazawa sitting like a statue behind the steering wheel of his car, and from the waist down he felt like one of Mom's jiggly gelatin salads.

Lunchtime conversations now and then would be good. Or a chat while walking to and from class. If he had that with Millie, he'd be the happiest ninth grader at Grover Cleveland High. She had a lot of interesting things to say, and according to her, he was very good at listening.

He left the cafeteria feeling as though he were walking on a cloud of Mr. Farber's helium. Floating.

CHAPTER FIFTEEN

fter science the next day, Mr. Farber asked Melvin to stay behind.

"Catch up with you later," Lenny said. He saluted their teacher. "Mr. Farber, another fine lesson. You make electromagnetism absolutely mesmerizing." Melvin agreed silently, wishing those big words could flow as easily from his tongue.

Mr. Farber nodded, then sat and pointed to another stool. They faced each other across the demonstration counter at the front of the room. "So, how's high school treating you so far?"

It had been almost three weeks since school began, and with the exception of Gary's nearly daily taunts and not being able to voice his thoughts in class, Melvin supposed it was going all right. Also, did Mr. Farber plan to have a long chat? Melvin glanced at the clock. Only three minutes to get to choir.

"Don't worry. I'll write you a note. Who's your next teacher?"

Melvin tapped his leg, took a deep breath, and tried to exhale the *M*. "Mmmmmiss Guh-Gale, sir."

Sir was not a requirement in their school, but Pops stressed it for his own children, saying it would make them stand out among their peers if they used *ma'am* and *sir* when addressing their teachers.

"No problem, then. She's very understanding. You can relax."

He was only talking about not worrying about being late, but the encouragement to relax set off a chain reaction of feelings that bordered on hostility inside Melvin. How many times had people told him to relax while he was trying to get out his words? As if simply relaxing could solve the problem. *It didn't.*

"So, I've noticed you're having some troubles with your speech."

Melvin's gaze roamed to Mr. Farber's wooden arm. He found it interesting that the man always wore short-sleeved shirts, as if he wanted everyone to see that he had a prosthetic arm. If Melvin were in his position, he'd wear long sleeves.

"How long have you had a stutter?" he asked directly.

For as long as I can remember, Melvin thought. It had shown up when he started school, but it might as well have been with him his entire life.

"Sssssince I wuh-was ffffive . . . or around then."

Mr. Farber stayed quiet. Did he expect him to say more? Because Melvin didn't have anything else to say.

"You know it's not your fault . . . or, or some failure on your part that you stammer, right?"

Maybe it wasn't a failure, but it sure made him feel like one.

"You can't help it any more than I can help this."

Melvin looked up. Mr. Farber had his wooden arm in the air and was looking straight into Melvin's eyes. It was as if he'd been waiting for Melvin to make eye contact the whole time, as if he were a wire relaying a current of electricity. The man wouldn't look away until the current had jumped the gap between them.

"World War Two . . . if you were wondering. I was stationed in France for a while." He lowered his arm. "Listen, Melvin, my wife is a speech pathologist. If you're interested, and your parents approve, she could work with you."

Speech pathologist. Melvin had never heard of such a thing, although he could gather what one did.

"Puh-probably expensive."

"Don't need to worry about that. She would do it for free. I told her about you."

Melvin's face heated in embarrassment. "Nuh-nnnno." Inhale. Exhale. "Thank you." He wasn't a charity case. Pops had also drummed that into their heads. "Sssssir." He got up to go.

"Now, hold on, Melvin. There's no shame in accepting help. You think I didn't have to have some help when I was first getting used to this?" He lifted his hook again. "Just so you know, it's very common for stress to exacerbate a stutter. Starting high school is stressful. Add two older siblings who are highly accomplished . . ."

And a Rat who won't leave you alone, Melvin thought.

Mr. Farber looked at Melvin meaningfully. "Am I right?"

Melvin kept his eyes on the counter. He nodded once, reluctantly.

"At least think about it. My wife has had a lot of success with young people . . . and adults. People who've stuttered much longer than you."

Melvin swallowed. "Thank you for your—" He wanted to say *concern* but could feel his throat closing at the mere thought of the hard *C.* "Thank you."

Mr. Farber found a slip of paper and a pencil and scribbled a note—with the pencil in his hook. "These things can't stop us from doing what we want, Melvin." He looked Melvin in the eye again. "Unless we let them."

Melvin nodded. He was exhausted from the exchange, which had lasted all of six minutes. He hurried off to choir, wrestling with the yearning to find hope in Mr. Farber's offer and the fear that he couldn't be fixed.

* * *

When he got home that day he found Mom sitting with her elbow on the dining table, hand over her mouth, and the afternoon paper spread before her. He saw the headline, "Accused Murderers Acquitted in Case of Slain Negro Boy." He didn't need to read any further: he knew it was about Emmett Till. He set his books down. Thoughts of Mr. Farber's offer (which he'd been ruminating over all the way home) fell away.

Mom closed up the paper when she realized he was within distance to read the article. He wished she didn't feel the need to protect him from such things, and yet, part of him didn't want to know. Part of him wanted to go back to being a carefree kid, although, when had that ever been, really? The Stutter had made that pretty near impossible.

"Wwwwwill they be ssssent to jail?"

She looked at him as if his question had broken her heart in two. She shook her head. "I'm afraid not."

"Aren't they guh-guh-guilty?"

"All the evidence would say so."

"Hhhhhow does that hhhappen?"

"It's evil, Melvin. Evil turned good by consensus. It's people committed tooth and nail to protect themselves and their way of life from whomever they see as a threat—outsiders, 'intruders,' those they think aren't deserving like they are. Oh, they can couch it in some mighty fine words that sound smart, all right"—she was getting worked up—"even *holy*, Lord have mercy. Words like *inalienable rights* and *divine order*. But when it comes down to it, it's evil. Plain and simple." She stooped slightly, as if she shouldered a great weight.

Melvin walked to his bedroom in a fog. He sat at his desk and watched Tuck crawl onto his island. Melvin felt as if he'd lived his life on an island, isolated and unaware of the evil his mom had named. He was starting to wonder if this fear that caused some people to see others as threatening and ultimately less deserving was more common than he'd realized.

It made him wish he had a shell.

CHAPTER SIXTEEN

Melvin stared at his tongue in the bathroom mirror. He thought of the Bible verse Reverend Reed had preached on last Sunday: the tongue was the littlest of the body's members, and yet what havoc it could wreak! Melvin didn't need anyone to tell *him* that. The tongue was a fire, Reverend Reed had said, that set things around it ablaze. An unruly evil that no man could tame.

Melvin wouldn't accept that. He was going to tame his tongue— "come hell or high water," as Grandma Robinson would say. Mr. Feuchtinger said success lay in doing one's daily exercises, and Melvin had been doing them . . . maybe not every day, but most days. Chuck, who lifted weights in their garage while bellowing loud enough for people to hear him two counties over, would mock him if he heard Melvin say it, but exercising your tongue was hard work!

When he was finished, he slicked on a little pomade and slid a brush across his hair until his curls were nice and even. He smiled in the mirror. He had a nice smile, full of big, white, straight teeth. He imagined Millie was on the other side, returning his grin with one of her own shy ones. He was nice to talk to, she had said. He winked at his reflection and then walked to his bedroom, feeling fine. He had planned to pick up his accordion and keep on going, but Chuck stopped him.

"Where you off to?" Chuck was in his bunk, resting up before that night's game.

Should Melvin tell him? Normally, he wouldn't have, but since Chuck had been so concerned about his social status at Cleveland . . . Having a friend who lived at the Harlem Club—that was cool, right?

"Mmmy friend Luh-Lenny's." He paused. "Hhhe lives above the Harlem . . . Cuh-Club."

Chuck rolled onto his elbow, making his bicep bulge. How many times had Melvin wished he could have his brother's muscles or his strong jawline? He didn't even need to have both—just one of those, and he'd be happy. "The Harlem Club? Do Mom and Pops know?"

Melvin shook his head.

Chuck lay on his back again. "That's mighty brave of you, Melvin. Brave or stupid, I'm not sure which. But I'll keep it to myself. For now."

"Thanks. Sssee you later."

"Later."

Melvin grabbed his bike from the garage and straddled it in the driveway. He had never actually ridden his bike with his accordion case, but how hard could it be? He set the case on the front handlebars and pushed off, one hand on his accordion, the other trying to keep the handlebars from wobbling.

Pretty hard, it turned out.

He swerved left and right trying to find his balance, nearly impossible when half his strength was being used to keep the heavy case from falling. He reached the end of the driveway, looked left, and pulled up. Old Man Pritchard and his mangy, beat-down dog were coming his way. The man ambled, unsteady, weaving almost as badly as Melvin had on his bike. Melvin never liked encountering him, and when the man was with his dog it was even worse. *Much* worse.

Melvin's heart beat faster. A lump rose in his throat. He turned the front tire so it was facing in the right direction—*away* from the old man. His sweaty hands made holding on to the case even harder than it already had been.

"Nigger!" Old Man Pritchard shouted.

He wasn't yelling at Melvin. Not that that made it any better.

He was yelling at his dog. That was the dog's name.

Melvin glanced back. The dog raced toward him, teeth bared. Melvin's heart practically burst from his chest as he scrambled to get his bike moving again, but his case was unsteady and heavy and he couldn't move as fast as he wanted.

"Nigger, get back here!" the old man called again. At least he was calling the dog *back* and not siccing him on Melvin.

The dog was not listening.

Its barking grew louder. Melvin could practically feel the animal's jaws locking onto his ankle. He saw himself tumbling to the ground in a tangle of metal and fur, the dog lunging for his face, his throat. He threw his whole weight into the front pedal and the bike surged forward. His case almost fell, but he gripped it harder and pedaled for his life, hoping that by some miracle the dog would listen to his master and leave him alone.

He sped on, afraid to turn and look. His ragged breathing filled his ears. Ahead, the traffic signal was not in his favor. Turn green. Turn green. As if hearing his plea, the light changed. He raced past the library and zoomed through the intersection.

He braked on the other side. His accordion catapulted from the handlebars and skidded along the sidewalk. His chest heaved. He felt as if he'd just crossed a river while running from a bear, and now he was safe on the opposite shore. Unfortunately, the dog was not as lucky. Old Man Pritchard had caught the dog and kicked it again and again.

Melvin shakily dismounted and walked to where his case had come to rest. His limbs felt jangly, weak. He hoped his accordion hadn't broken. The rush of adrenaline over, it hit him how much he despised that old man. He had named his dog a hateful word to let Melvin's family know how he felt about them—without having to say it directly to their faces.

Melvin felt sorriest for the dog.

* * *

When he reached the Harlem Club, Melvin's pedaling slowed. The doors had already opened for dinner. The atmosphere outside was much different from when he had come after school. The parking lot and entrance buzzed, along with the "Dine-DANCE" sign on the roof.

Melvin was used to being around white people, of course, but after seeing the verdict in the Emmett Till case the day before, and talking to Mom about people banding together against those they considered a threat, he felt suddenly uncomfortable and outnumbered. If Lenny hadn't appeared at the side door and waved him in, he would likely have turned his bike around and headed home—in spite of the possibility that Old Man Pritchard and his dog were still roaming the neighborhood.

Lenny reached for the heavy case, which Melvin appreciated. He was tired of the balancing act. "What happened here?" Lenny pointed to the fresh scrape along one side of the brown leather. Melvin hadn't taken time to examine it after the fall. It was pretty bad.

"I duh-dropped it." He didn't feel the need to go into details.

One of Lenny's eyebrows slid up; the other went down, like stair steps. "You sure you didn't drop *kick* it?"

"Wwwwhere should I puh-park my bike?"

"Right outside.the door is fine." Lenny turned and went into the vestibule. Melvin joined him on the stairs. "Seriously. What happened?"

"Nnnnothing. Really."

"If you say so. Looks like you were taking out some aggressions."

Yeah, there was some aggression, all right. Just not mine.

Melvin followed Lenny into his room and sat on his bed.

"You sure you're okay?" Lenny asked. He pulled out a few albums from the cabinet below his record player. "You seem kind of distracted."

Melvin didn't feel like talking about Old Man Pritchard and his dog, but Lenny was right. His mind was on something else. "Thhhhat buh-boy, Emmett Tuh-Till. The men were ffffound nuh-not guilty."

Lenny sat next to him on the bed. The album in his hands featured Louis Armstrong. Lenny stayed quiet for an unusually long time. "They did it, didn't they?"

Melvin nodded, squinting.

"Sorry, Melvin. That's not right."

Melvin reached for the album and Lenny handed it over. Melvin told him what he had learned from Grandma Robinson about Mr. Armstrong's visit to Spokane. How Negro families had put up the famous trumpet player and his band for the night, how his grandma had danced with him, and of course about the toilet sitting in her basement. They laughed about that.

"Ready to play?" Lenny asked.

Melvin snapped open his case, examined his accordion. It looked okay. He gave Lenny a thumbs-up.

"All right then, let's blow!"

They ran through "It Don't Mean a Thing" a few times. With each repetition Melvin's fingers felt a little more agile, a little more like they knew where to land on the buttons. He liked playing with Lenny, and he had to admit, they sounded good together. The hum of the accordion provided a solid foundation for the saxophone's rising and falling notes, like a channel holding the flowing water of a river.

It was a new experience to play music with another person. He'd only ever played his accordion on his own, and that as little as he could. Mr. Javanovich was always scolding him for not being better prepared for his weekly lesson. Playing on his own was boring. Playing with Lenny was fun—challenging, but fun. Or maybe fun because it *was* challenging.

They listened to an album called *The Battle of Birdland* featuring Sonny Stitt and Eddie "Lockjaw" Davis, who dueled with their saxophones. After that, Lenny got Melvin to improvise like the musicians on the album. Melvin had never played something that wasn't written down. They took turns "speaking" to each other in eight-measure sentences. It took Melvin several tries to feel comfortable moving beyond the same four-note pattern, but slowly he began to add notes, change rhythms. He was communicating—without needing to open his mouth or spit out a single syllable.

"We sound good!" Lenny exclaimed when they were done. "I'm telling you, we could win *Starlit Stairway*. We're just as good as anyone I've ever seen on there."

Melvin thought they *could* be, but they weren't yet.

"Sooo . . . Millie?" Lenny waggled his eyebrows.

Melvin's insides jumped at the unexpected mention of her name.

Lenny eyed Melvin from behind his glasses. "You're asking her to the Homecoming Dance, obviously."

Melvin's tongue went rigid. He played an F minor, then an E minor chord. No way. In case Lenny didn't catch his meaning, he shook his head.

"Why not?"

"I'm a hhhhorrible dancer, a buh-buh-bad cuh—" He took a breath. "Cuh-conversational-*list*, and mmmost of all, her dad scares me. Also, I hhhave no wuh-way to get her there. We don't drive, remember?"

"One of your parents can drop you off."

"Embarrassing."

"Chuck, then."

"Wwworse."

"Well, you like her, don't you?"

"Ye-a-ah," he said slowly.

"So you should ask her." Lenny slicked back his thick hair with one hand.

Melvin sat there, the accordion heavy on his lap. Lenny's conclusion was reasonable. He liked her. He should ask her. But if he was honest, the reason he didn't plan to ask her wasn't any of the ones he had said. He didn't want to hear her say no. Or rather, "No, thank you," which is what Millie would say because she was polite.

He tapped the side of his accordion quickly. "Wuh-what if she says nnnno?"

"What if she says yes?"

He exhaled. "Exactly. Wuh-what if she says yyyyyes?"

Lenny blew into his horn. Out came a sultry string of notes that said, It will be the night of your life.

Melvin played back tentatively: I'll consider it. The chord at the end didn't resolve.

The sound of drums and horns reverberated in the air. The Thirteen Black Cats had started their first set.

Lenny grinned. "Come on, we'll go listen. After I take care of my mouthpiece." He went to work disassembling and cleaning his saxophone.

Melvin watched with interest. The saxophone had a mouth too.

"Need to replace my reed soon. This one's chipped." Lenny removed the thin wooden piece that vibrated to generate sound.

Same as vocal cords, Melvin thought. If only it were as easy to swap parts of *his* mouthpiece for ones that worked.

Lenny closed his instrument in its case. "Let's go take in some music!"

Melvin checked the clock on the nightstand. Six straight up. "I c—" He took a deep breath. "I . . . *cuh-can't.*"

"You gotta go home for dinner or something? Eat here! Ma will feed you."

It hit Melvin like a kick to the windpipe. He was not allowed, for the exact same reason that Louis Armstrong had been turned away from the city's hotels. He shook his head and stared at Lenny, waiting for him to get it. It was Saturday night, not Sunday or Monday.

Deep lines appeared between Lenny's eyebrows. Then a look of puzzlement. Finally, his eyes widened; his jaw went slack. "Oh." There was an awkward silence, but it didn't last long. "Aw, come on. Mr. Jones won't mind. You're my friend. You're part of the mish-pachah now."

But Melvin minded. He wasn't looking to cause any trouble. And he didn't like the idea of having to sneak around, trying to avoid being seen by the white customers, just because he wasn't white. "Mmmaybe on a Sunday. I—" But no more sound was coming. He set his accordion down. "Cuh-cuh-can I leave this here?" He wanted to ride fast, without the extra weight.

"Sure. Leave it as long as you want. We'll practice every time you come over. Every day if you want." Melvin headed for the door but Lenny grabbed him by the shoulder. "I'm sorry, Mel. *Really.*"

Melvin knew he meant it, but still, it was weird, this feeling that he couldn't do what Lenny could, just because they were different colors. He had never had that happen. Spokane wasn't Mississippi, after all. But hadn't Pops told them? There was a wall here too.

And Melvin had just run into it.

CHAPTER SEVENTEEN

Melvin rode home in the dark. He'd been shaken by how his time at the Harlem Club had ended, for sure, but being barred from that place had sparked something inside. Something unfamiliar. Was it courage? Determination?

Pedaling down the sidewalk, his mind repeated one word and one word only: *Millie. Millie. Millie.* Even the thought of crossing Old Man Pritchard and his dog again didn't scare him. He was a man on a mission.

He passed his house, where light from inside reflected off the Jessups' car in the driveway. Two more cars were out front. It was his parents' week to host their card-playing friends for bridge club.

He dropped his bike in the front yard and set his face toward the white house across the street, a few doors down. He took a deep breath and crossed Empire Avenue, giving himself a pep talk along the way.

You can do this! You talked to her at school. You can do it again. She's nice. She's not thrown off by the Stutter. You can do this!

On the Takazawas' front porch his breathing turned shallow; his throat began to constrict. What if Mr. Takazawa answered the door?

He recalled the words of Mr. Feuchtinger: "The super-voice begins in the brain and not in the throat."

Good evening, he practiced silently. In his brain, his voice was a deep baritone. *Good evening. Is Millie home?*

In his brain, his voice flowed as easily as the Spokane River. In his brain, he wasn't a stutterer. So how did he get from in his brain to talking to Millie without stumbling?

If his younger sister happened to look out their front window, which she was prone to do, she would see him standing there looking like a dummy. Better hurry up. He knocked quickly, practically jumping at the sound of his own knuckles. The echo seemed to fill the deserted street. He glanced over his shoulder, expecting to see Maisy peering out, curious about who was knocking on a neighbor's door after dark. He panicked.

Is it too late at night to make a neighborly call?

The door cracked open. It was Mrs. Takazawa. Melvin had never actually spoken to the woman, although they'd once entered Berto's Butchery at the same time. Melvin had motioned for her to place her order first, out of respect. She had nodded and smiled her approval. She smiled the same way right then. "Hello . . . Melvin, am I right?"

He nodded.

"Are you looking for Millie?"

More nodding. He was afraid she would think him rude, but he couldn't find his breath.

"Mi-chan!" she called. "There is someone here to see you."

A moment later Millie appeared. Her eyes sparkled. He thought of the sun shining on Curlew Lake. "Hello, Melvin! How are you?"

He drummed his fingers like crazy. He couldn't let Mrs. Takazawa think he was not fit for her daughter before he even had a chance to prove himself. "Fffffine."

Mrs. Takazawa spoke: "Would you like to come in?"

"Yes, thank you." He told himself his tongue was flexible, strong, and supple. It could rival Chuck's bicep any day.

Millie beckoned him to the settee in the front room. She sat on the nearby couch. Her mom asked if they would like some tea.

"Nuh-no, thank you," he replied, feeling better by the moment. Maybe his tongue push-ups were working after all!

"Well, I'll be in the kitchen if you two need anything." She smiled sweetly at them.

Melvin glanced at Millie. Her shiny hair was parted on the side, held back with a clip. She wore a V-neck sweater with pearls for buttons. It made her long and lovely neck look even longer and lovelier. Don't stare at her neck!

He needed somewhere else to focus. He surveyed the room.

A stand-up radio. A smallish television on a table. A short shelf of books. A black upright piano.

"Is your dad hhhhere?" Even though he was feeling pretty good, not knowing whether the stern-looking man would appear at any moment was testing his nerves.

"No, he's on a trip."

Relief washed over him; he relaxed completely. His tongue was so tenderized it was practically filet mignon.

His eyes roamed to what looked like a memorial, atop the short bookshelf. A framed picture of a young man in a military uniform was surrounded by fruit and lit candles. It made him think of the framed pictures he'd seen of Uncle Melvin after he was killed. A medallion on a ribbon was draped over the photo. "Whhho is that?"

"My brother," Millie said. "He died . . . in the Korean War."

"Oh." There was really nothing more that could be said, but he added an "I'm sorry," because he was. Even though he and Chuck didn't always see eye to eye, Melvin would still never want his brother to die in a war.

"My parents will never get over it. They dug out a pond in our backyard, a place to go and remember him. It's one of my favorite places to be. You'll have to come back in the daytime to see it."

Melvin tried not to smile too big at the idea, even though her invitation made him ecstatic.

Something else caught his eye—a vase on top of the piano. It was riddled through with cracks, as if it had been broken into a dozen or more pieces, and then someone had put it back together again. Not with any old glue, however. The cracks had been filled with gold. The glinting veins ran up, down, and around the vase like tributaries of a river on a map, holding the pieces together and giving the vessel an appearance that he suspected was even more beautiful than the original, unbroken version.

"It was my grandmother's," Millie said. "She was from Japan."

He'd been staring at it for a while, he realized with a start.

"It got broken when my parents were packing up all of our belongings, trying to find some place to store everything while we were away . . ." She continued quietly, "In the camp . . . the prison."

He said, "It's . . . buh-beautiful," and then added silently, like you. He hoped she couldn't read minds.

"My mom swept up the pieces and kept them with her. If it hadn't broken, the vase would likely have been lost or sold. But she kept the pieces the whole time, and when we got out, my great-uncle made this. He's a master kintsugi craftsman."

Melvin felt his brow furrow.

"Kintsugi," she repeated, comprehending him perfectly without words. "The craftsmen take broken pottery and remake it with precious metals as the mortar—so it's even stronger than before."

He saw that the vase was no longer just a vase. It had become something more because of what it had gone through.

There was silence between them. It was getting longer . . . and longer. Now! he shouted at himself. Ask her now!

"Did you see *Starlit Stairway* tonight?" she asked.

The mention of the show out of nowhere surprised him. He shook his head, feeling a heaviness settle into his chest. He had blown a perfectly good chance to invite her to the dance!

"It was a really good one."

He raised his eyebrows in interest.

She leaned forward to tell him more. "A girl with flaming batons accidentally set the backdrop on fire!" She covered her laughing mouth as Melvin's dropped open.

"The firemen must have been watching the show, because they got there faster than humanly possible. It was out in a matter of minutes and no one was hurt. All on live television! Can you believe it?"

"Did she wwwwin?"

"She almost burned the station down! *No!*"

He shrugged.

"She didn't win, but no one's going to forget her act anytime soon—maybe ever!"

He said it before he could stop himself: "Luh-Lenny wwwants mmme to go on there with him." Mentioning the possibility of being on television made him feel a little bigger, after his failure to bring up the dance.

"Oh, Melvin, that would be amazing!"

Millie would be impressed if he went on *Starlit Stairway*?

Now he *had* to do it.

CHAPTER EIGHTEEN

Melvin walked back to his house not completely dejected. He hadn't gotten up the nerve to ask her— *yet*—but they had had another friendly conversation, and in her own living room! He was greasing the skids, working his way up to it. The next time they were together, no matter what, he would ask her to the dance.

He picked up his bike and walked it down the driveway. He'd planned to slip in the back door unnoticed, but Bubba was sitting at the top of the steps, his chin resting in the bowl of his fleshy hand. Bubba might have a round baby face, but he was the first of any of Melvin's friends, including Melvin himself, to have the faintest hint of hair growing on his upper lip. "Finally!" he said, sitting up. "What took you so long?"

"I—" He hadn't really considered when he would tell Bubba about the Harlem Club, but he might as well go ahead. He trusted Bubba more than Chuck, and he'd told Chuck.

"Never mind," Bubba said. "You're here now. You wouldn't believe how much the adults in there been going on about Homecoming. Haven't stopped talking about it since they walked in the door. I think we're in trouble."

Melvin climbed the steps and sat next to him. "Wwwwhat do you mmmean?"

"I mean, I think we're being set up!"

Set up? Melvin stared at his best buddy, waiting for him to explain.

"My mom was the worst." Bubba spoke in a high falsetto voice: "In the same year that Marian Anderson became the first Negro to perform at the Metropolitan Opera House, *our* Marian is the first in Spokane to become a Homecoming Princess! Isn't it *marvelous?*" He grinned and clapped with glee, apparently imitating Mrs. Jessup. A grimace replaced the smile. "I wouldn't be surprised if my dad took out his betting notebook and started taking wagers on whether she wins Homecoming Queen. I'm happy for your sister and all, but geez, why are they making such a big deal?"

A week ago—even just a few days ago—Melvin might have had the same response. But after Mrs. Stimson's reaction to the news about Emmett Till (and then the murderers getting off scot-free), and learning about Spokane's finest hotel rejecting Louis Armstrong, and his own still-fresh experience at the Harlem Club . . . he was starting to understand.

At various times he'd overheard women at his parents' bridge club talking about slights they'd received from white store clerks, or men discussing the lack of job opportunities, or all of them wishing there was even *one* Negro dentist in town.

The Wall.

He recalled something Maisy had told him the other day. Shyla had written to her about a town down South—*a whole town*—that was built by Negroes, and everyone who lived there was Negro. All the teachers, and doctors, and firefighters were all Negroes too.

"Can you imagine that?" Grandma had said when she'd heard about it. Melvin couldn't really. Spokane didn't have a single Negro firefighter, police officer, or doctor, and there was only *one* Negro teacher in the entire city, at Lewis and Clark High.

"They've puh-puh-protected us."

"Huh? What are you talking about?"

"I overheard MMMrs. Dalbert tuh-talking to my mom . . . Her dentist asked her not to cuh-come back. A wwwwwhite woman cuh-complained that she made her uncomfortable, in the wwww-waiting room."

"That's bad. But what's that got to do with Marian being Homecoming Princess?"

Melvin knew there was a connection but he didn't know if he could put it into words, and he was mad that his mouth wasn't cooperating better. He imagined he was holding his accordion. How would he say it in music? "They've llllived longer. Ssssseeen more. Buh-buh-but they don't tuh-talk about these things to *us*. They tuh-talk to each other. I think they want to puh-puh-protect us."

Bubba's head tilted back. He fixed Melvin with his gaze. "I wasn't wanting to say anything, but . . . I haven't heard you stutter this bad for a while. You okay, man?"

Melvin's forehead scrunched. He looked at his shoes. He and Bubba had grown up together. Their dads had grown up together before them. Melvin could tell him anything, but he didn't know what to say.

He shrugged. "Mmmmy science tuh-teacher says it mmmmight buh-buh-be high school, you know, ssss . . . stress." He hated how the Stutter made him feel short of breath.

Bubba shrugged. "Don't make no difference to me. I just thought I should ask. Didn't want you to be thinking it bothered me."

Melvin gave him a quick nod.

"So is Cleveland that bad?"

Melvin laughed. "It's all right. How's Ssssaint Xavier's?"

"Strict, man. Those nuns don't mess around. And the students . . . *woo-ee!* They got the foulest mouths of anyone I ever heard. Those white boys be cussin' every chance they get."

That cracked Melvin up. Music floated out from the kitchen windows, which Mom always opened when the house was full of guests, even in the dead of winter, because of how hot it got in their small house.

Some of the men started to sing along. "May-be-llene! Why can't you be true?" It had been one of the most popular songs of the summer, sung by a Negro performer named Chuck Berry, who was taking the charts by storm. White kids had been raving about his music as much as anyone.

"Must be time for the dance break," Bubba said. "Let's go get some of them mints."

Inside, the dining table was laid out with silver trays of deviled eggs and tiny sandwiches that made Melvin wonder, Why bother? He and Bubba grabbed handfuls of cocktail peanuts and the pink and green mints, and shoved them in their mouths. The adults were in the living room cutting a rug, as Mom liked to say, and from the ruckus in the basement, Maisy and Bubba's two younger brothers were down there playing with Pops's train set. Mikey's and Ant-Ant's whoops and hollers were as loud as the music.

A bottle of bourbon sat out surrounded by glass tumblers. Bubba pointed to the liquor and raised his eyebrows, as if to ask, Should we?

Melvin shook his head emphatically. Pops had given him a taste of that stuff when Melvin was around ten years old. He'd spit most of it into the sink, with the strength and speed of a firehose, but some had gone down his throat. It burned so bad he thought he'd never talk again.

"When did *you* get here?" Mom entered the room so suddenly, Melvin jumped in his shoes. He felt guilty even though he hadn't done a thing except *look* at the liquor. She kissed him on the cheek. "Have a good time at your friend's house?"

His conscience was pricked again, although this time he actually was hiding something—where Lenny lived. He ignored the guilt and nodded. He *had* had a good time, in spite of facing the reality that while Lenny and the others were hospitable, in the club itself he hadn't been welcome at all.

"You'll have to have Lenny over to *our* house next time. Maybe the three of you can get together," she said, indicating Bubba. She grabbed Melvin's arm. "Now that you're here, we can talk about this dance coming up."

"Duh-dance?" Melvin asked, feeling suddenly nervous.

"Homecoming, of course!" She laughed gaily.

Bubba raised skeptical eyebrows and smirked. He whispered the word "Setup."

Mom led Melvin into the living room, where seven grown adults were acting like *they* were at a high school dance. The record player must have been on repeat because they still bopped and twisted to "Maybellene."

"Claude, turn that off for a minute," Mom shouted to Pops. He lifted the needle off the record and everyone slowly came to a standstill. "Boys," Mom said, piercing Melvin with a look so intent it set his brow to sweating. "We've been talking, and we've got it all figured out."

Melvin had a bad feeling about where this was headed. Any time adults said they had something "all figured out," it was time to run for the hills.

"Between our families, there are three high school girls who need dates to the Homecoming Dance, and there are three of you. Chuck has agreed to escort Marian, our representative on the *royal* court . . ."

Hold up! Melvin wanted to shout. She couldn't just set him up with one of her friends' daughters! But she had. *They* had. She said they'd been talking! Making plans completely without his say-so.

"Bubba will escort Miss Sylvia Purcell."

Not bad, Melvin thought. Sylvia was tall and pretty. Too tall for Melvin, but just right for Bubba.

"And Melvin, you will take Eugenia, the Dalberts' daughter."

Melvin felt his eyes bug. Eugenia was a *senior*!

Dignified Mrs. Dalbert tipped her head, smiling. Squat Mr. Dalbert looked like he was playing poker—no expression.

Melvin stood there, stunned.

No, thank you! he silently asserted, but it was eight against one. The adults had gone back to laughing and chatting and were taking their seats around the card tables.

Would Millie have said yes? Now he would never know. He was going to the Homecoming Dance with sturdy, nerdy Eugenia Dalbert.

CHAPTER NINETEEN

fter church the next day, Maisy tried to convince him to go to Grandma's to work on the basement with her, even though he'd already told her he was done. That film in social studies had sealed the deal: Grandma had hired them for a fool's errand.

"Anyway, it's the Lord's Day," he told Maisy with a sly grin. "We have to rest. Holy Bible says so." His mouth felt loose. Maybe the exercises were working, or maybe he was just having a good day. It was hard to tell.

Maisy picked up Melvin's pillow and threw it at him. "Fine by me. But don't expect me to bring you any ginger ale."

"Would you two pipe down?" Chuck said. He was sitting at their desk, hunched over his math book and a pad of paper. He returned to his computations. Maisy stuck out her tongue at his back.

"Juh-just don't fffforget the . . . the you-know-what," he whispered.

"I know, I know. The photo." She stalked out of the room. In truth, Melvin didn't plan to sit around doing nothing. He'd been putting off writing a book report all weekend. He leaned back against his Wall of Wonders and got to work.

When Maisy got home, Melvin was in the kitchen pouring himself a glass of milk. She grabbed his arm and pulled him through the dining area. He set the milk on the table as they passed. She still had ahold of him and he almost spilled it. "Hey! What's the rush?"

She led him out the back door and around the side of the house. "I found something amazing!" She reached into the bag slung across her shoulder and pulled out the photo of Pops and the boy. "That's not what I'm talking about, of course." He pocketed the picture while she reached in again for whatever had gotten her so worked up.

Melvin expected to see something like a giant ruby ring or a handful of magic beans, the way his sister was acting. Instead, she pulled out a leather-bound book tied shut with a thin leather strip. "I found Pops's diaries."

Did boys keep diaries?

"There was more than one. But in *this* one . . ." She opened the book to a dog-eared page. "In this one, he talks about how he's going to be a journalist, Melvin. A journalist! Just like me."

Pops worked for the postal service, not a newspaper. And he'd never talked about being a writer either, although he revered the Bard as much as Mom did the Holy Bible. They'd fought so much over whether their kids would have Bible- or Shakespeare-inspired middle names, they'd all gotten one of each. Thus, Melvin James Horatio Robinson. Charles Paul Duncan. Marian Esther Hermia. And Margaret (Maisy) Ruth Juliet.

"Wonder what happened," Melvin said.

Maisy's eyebrows pulled together like charcoal smudges. "Oh, Melvin. It's so terrible. He wrote about the whole thing. Here." She pointed to the page.

Melvin scanned Pops's cursive. The handwriting was so perfect, it looked like it'd been lifted right out of the Constitution of the United States of America. The entry was from November 1, 1929. Melvin did the math. Pops would have been eighteen, a senior in high school.

He wrote about how his plans to be the first in his family to go to college had come crashing down—the same day as the stock market. All of his savings had been lost. He would be going to work to help feed his brothers.

Melvin remembered hearing in school about the great stock market crash of 1929 that had led to hard times for most people in the country. It had been so bad they'd called it the Depression. He had no idea that it had affected Pops like this.

"Isn't it awful?" Maisy whispered. "I feel so badly for him. He had dreams, Melvin, just like you and me."

More like you, Melvin thought. There was more to the entry, so Melvin read on.

"Ariel offered to give me a loan. He kept his money at home, not at the bank, and has enough to cover my first year . . ."

Ariel? Who was Ariel? Melvin had never heard Pops mention the name, but whoever he was, he had made a very generous offer.

". . . but I must refuse. I have an obligation to my family, and my personal pursuits and ambitions must be put aside. Maybe for a time, maybe forever. Also, I will not be in debt to any man."

Wow. Pops had made a huge sacrifice for his family, and never mentioned it once. He was still making sacrifices, going to work at a place that wasn't his first choice, for Melvin and his brother and sisters. Melvin wanted to make Pops' sacrifices worth it. He wanted to make him proud—but how? He was just Melvin, stuck in the middle between talented and socially skilled Marian and Chuck on one side, and outgoing and ambitious Maisy on the other.

The boy whom God had overlooked.

* * *

The flurry of excitement around Marian's nomination to the Homecoming Court only intensified the following week. Turned out, the school's boosters (alumni and other supporters) hosted a fundraising dinner every year before Homecoming, and they always invited the Princesses to attend as special guests.

Mom spent every waking moment of that week sewing a new dress for Marian, so even if Melvin hadn't asked her permission, she likely wouldn't have noticed that he went over to Lenny's every day to rehearse. Now that they were for sure auditioning for *Starlit Stairway*, he wanted to be as prepared as possible. He had to impress Millie!

He'd gotten *so* wrapped up in practicing, he had forgotten about asking Pops about the photograph, but Friday he came home from Lenny's with the picture on his mind.

He found the photo in his desk drawer and went to the living room where Pops was reading. Pops looked up and Melvin held out the picture. "Found this at Grandma's. Wwwwas wondering . . . who it is."

Pops held the picture, silent. "Huh. That's my friend, Ariel. Don't know if I've ever seen this picture."

Ariel. The person who had offered Pops the loan after he lost his savings. It had to be. Of course, Melvin couldn't let on that he knew anything about that. Didn't want Pops to think they were snooping in his private business, even though they had been.

"Wwwhat's he hhholding?"

"It had something to do with his Jewish religion. That particular day they'd had some kind of special celebration. I went over to his house afterward. We were around thirteen, I believe. Same age as you."

Lenny had told him that when a Jewish boy turned thirteen it was a big deal. He had called it something . . . bar-something?

Pops tapped the picture on his fingertips. "Well, thanks for showing me this. Brings back some good memories." He handed it back to Melvin.

Melvin returned the photo to the darkness of his desk drawer, briefly wondering what had happened to this once strong friendship. He supposed that's the way it went with friends, especially early-on ones. He and Lenny would likely go the same way, eventually.

* * *

Saturday night was the boosters' dinner, downtown at the fancy Davenport Hotel. When Marian left the house with Pops, you would have thought she was leaving on a ship to cross the ocean. Mom wouldn't stop messing with Marian's dress and her hair, and after they were out the back door, Mom and Maisy ran to the front porch to wave and blow kisses at Big Bertha as she pulled out onto Empire Avenue.

Melvin turned to Chuck where they sat on the couch watching TV. "Aren't they buh-being a lllllittle over the tuh-top?"

Chuck shrugged. "It's a big deal for her. And for us."

He knew his brother was right. But still.

On TV, two ladies were acting the fool, running around and shouting at each other. One was named Lucy. The other was Ethel.

They were throwing pies in each other's faces. Melvin chuckled. Crazy white people.

They watched television until the networks signed off. Melvin was brushing his teeth for bed when Pops came back from picking up Marian. The sound of Mom's excited greeting dropped off abruptly. Marian and Maisy's bedroom door closed louder than usual for that time of night. Melvin rinsed his mouth and went into the living room, wiping his face with the hand towel. Mom and Pops stood in the kitchen, talking in strained tones. Marian was nowhere in sight.

"Sounds like she ran into some trouble at the hotel," Pops was saying.

"What do you mean? What kind of trouble?" Mom's voice was high and tight.

Melvin crept forward. He didn't want to be told to go to his room. Pops spied him. His jaw tensed. He continued, "Some hotel employee told her she had to ride the freight elevator up to the event. Couldn't get in the regular elevator with the other girls."

Mom's eyes took on a fire Melvin had never seen. Like she was plotting to hurt someone. Then just as sudden, her chest caved in like a big sinkhole. Her hands flew up to cover the crumbling of her stony facade. Pops held her in his arms as her body shuddered with sobs. "No, no, no," she moaned. When she straightened, her face was covered with tears.

Melvin stepped forward with the hand towel. She took it and wiped her face.

"Why?" she asked in a way that was clearly not meant to be answered. "*Why*, Claude?"

"You know I got no answers. We've proven over and over again we're every bit as good. *Better* because we've endured this treatment for centuries. Don't make no difference to them."

"I'll go talk to her," Mom said, but Pops held her arm.

"Two of the girls rode up with her," he said, and Mom put her hand to her heart. She composed herself and walked toward his sisters' room, tall and stately. Regal, even.

Pops turned to him. "Head on to bed now, son." Pops looked more tired than Melvin felt, but he did as he was told and went to his room. Chuck snored softly, protected by slumber.

Melvin wished he could rest as easily, but the Wall had appeared again, and this time it had hurt his sister. He was too angry to sleep.

CHAPTER TWENTY

The following Saturday morning, Mom dropped Melvin and Lenny off downtown in front of the two-story brick building that housed KXLY studios, home of *Starlit Stairway*. But not before she hugged and kissed on Melvin for so long he was afraid an officer would roll up and give them a ticket for double-parking.

"Have fun, you two," Mom said. She smiled at Lenny in the back seat.

"We will! Thanks for the ride, Mrs. Robinson," Lenny said as he got out of the car.

"You're welcome!" She turned to Melvin. "What a polite young man. I'm so glad you've become friends. Now listen, call me as *soon* as you know if you made it."

Melvin was pretty sure his mom was more excited about this opportunity than he was. "I wwwwwill, Mmmmom."

"And don't you worry none about speaking to that show host. What's his name?"

"Duh-duh-duh-*Dean*—"

"Right. Dean Dougherty. That man. I got all the ladies praying, and also, it don't matter, Melvin. No matter *what* happens. Just play your heart out, like I know you can. We're all so proud of you!" She kissed his cheek one last time.

"Mom, I've guh-got to *go!*"

"Okay, okay. Go, then!" She nudged him.

Melvin stepped out of the car and shut its heavy door. He had his accordion case in one hand, and his best and only Sunday suit in a garment bag slung over his shoulder. Mom waved like crazy, and he lifted his case in return. He and Lenny walked into the building together. He actually felt like a musician. Like one of the Thirteen Black Cats headed to a gig!

"Thanks for wuh-walking over this morning," he said. Lenny had shown up at their front door, to Mom's surprise. She'd assumed they'd be picking Lenny up. But Melvin had made sure that wouldn't happen.

"No problem," Lenny said. "Whatever it takes so you can keep coming over to my place."

Before Lenny arrived, Millie had appeared at their front door to *Melvin's* surprise. Shock, really. She'd given him a yellow-gold flower, a lily, she'd said, from her parents' greenhouse. For luck, she'd said. *A lily for luck.* He had been rendered speechless, and not because of the Stutter. He just didn't have any words. But he did know that if by some slim chance he got on television, Millie would think he was amazing.

The lady at the reception desk was friendly but businesslike. She showed them where to sign in and pointed in the direction of the double doors that would lead to the studio at the far end of a hall. When they pushed through the doors, Melvin's heart started banging against his ribs, as if it wanted out to catch the first bus home. Melvin agreed with his heart. The hallway was *packed* with kids and their parents, all apparently awaiting their chance to be on television.

He would've turned around and walked straight back through the double doors, if her name hadn't started up in his head again: *Millie. Millie. Millie.* He stuck by Lenny's side until a man with a clipboard appeared.

"All right, kids, it's time to get started. Follow me." He went through a door with the word *Studio* painted on it.

The crowd moved together: a boy with an instrument case like Lenny's, but smaller; a boy and girl who looked like brother and sister, wearing color-coordinated clothing and carrying small balls and what looked like bowling pins. Were they going to bowl for their talent? Four little girls in sequin-lined skirts and tap shoes clicked along in front of him. He was most intrigued by the boy who carried a mouse in a cage. The man with him held a large lidded box. Melvin was so curious he forgot about his own nervousness for a few moments and followed them into the studio just to see what the boy's talent would be.

The studio was basically a stage, where bright lights shone on the performance area and black curtains hid everything else behind the scenes. They filed through the dark, curtained area and into a large space in front of the stage. There it was—the famous backdrop against which kids performed their acts—newly repaired after the recent fire incident. Melvin had seen it many times on TV but never knew its true color because the picture was in black and white.

Yellow. So bright it practically hurt to look at it, like the Spokane summer sun. The words *Starlit* and *Stairway* hung on either side of a large central star that read *Boyle Fuel*, the sponsor of the show. Crisscrossing lines and more stars, gold and glittery, filled out the space. One read *Aberdeen Coal* and another *Caterized Oil*. On television it looked as good as the *Ed Sullivan Show*. Up close, it was honestly a little corny.

Melvin stood there uncomfortably. He and Lenny seemed to be the only ones carrying extra clothes. Everyone else was in their performance outfits. People glanced around, not really making eye contact. Only Lenny was saying hi to people he didn't know. Three men huddled around a table, looking at a list. Finally, one of them turned and faced the crowd.

"Good morning, everyone! Please take a seat out in the audience chairs there." Melvin and Lenny found seats. Melvin put his performance clothes over the back of a chair and set his case on the ground. "I'm Bud Byrd, the producer. These are my associates, Carny Wyborn, artistic director, and Phil Novak, cameraman. We'll get started in just a moment. We're waiting for the host—"

A man appeared from the wings in a plaid jacket and white loafers. "Did someone say my name?" He spread his arms wide and grinned even wider. Melvin would have recognized him anywhere.

"Actually, I didn't," the first man mumbled. "But now that you're here . . . Ladies and gentlemen, I give you Dean Dougherty, the *host* of *Starlit Stairway!*"

Everyone applauded, including Melvin. He was seeing a real live celebrity, up close and personal! Wait until he told Maisy. She would go bananas.

One by one, acts were called onto the set to perform. The three men and Dean Dougherty sat behind the table, watching and making notes. When performers finished, the man who'd first ushered them through the door led them back out.

The boy with the mouse was Melvin's favorite, by far. He had trained the mouse to do pirouettes on its hind legs. The mouse also set off a contraption that the boy had made, which turned on a lamp at the end. (That's what had been in the box!)

Melvin sat and watched patiently, swallowing every few moments, both to get rid of the saliva flooding his mouth and to try and keep his tongue loose, just in case he got called on to speak. Please don't make me talk, please don't make me talk. He hoped God was listening.

When Mr. Byrd called their names, Melvin's heart started pounding again. Let me outta here!

Lenny responded, "We're the Swingin' Saxoccordions, sir."

The man looked up from his list. "Say again?"

"The Swingin' Saxoccordions."

"All right, then. Come on up and show us what you've got, Swingin' Saxoccordions. Are you wearing what you're going to perform in?"

"No, sir," Lenny said. "Saving our outfits for later. Don't want to get them dirty before the show." He grinned.

Lenny was so confident. Melvin, on the other hand, was sweating so badly he was afraid his fingers would slip right off the keys. He gripped his accordion tightly and followed Lenny onto the floor in front of the yellow backdrop. Lenny took his time, puffing air through his horn, clearing it of debris and spit, as he always did before playing.

Dean Dougherty tapped the eraser end of his pencil rapidly on the paper in front of him. Melvin glanced at Lenny; his head was bowed, eyes closed. Was he praying? Melvin's breathing became rapid and shallow. He felt light-headed. He drew in a big breath and exhaled long and slow. Get a hold of yourself! He had to stay upright—he had to do this—for Millie.

"Whenever you're ready," Mr. Byrd said.

Melvin held his accordion steady in front of his chest, but it was getting heavy.

Lenny gave the count: "One, two, a one-two-three-four . . ."

And they were off, like the horses at Playfair, where Pops sometimes took him to place bets. They filled the studio with their unique sound. Lenny's sax was smooth and powerful, like a champion stallion. Melvin did his best to gallop along with him, but he felt himself falling behind, or maybe Lenny was rushing in his excitement. Either way, they weren't completely in sync. Melvin cut a chord short so they'd be back together.

Doo-wat, doo-wat, doo-wat, doo-wat, doo-wat, doo-wat, doo-wat, doo-wahhhhh, he sang in his head. His fingers switched chords with every *doo-wat*. His toes started tapping. He saw Lenny out of the corner of his eye. Lenny leaned toward him on one *doo-wat* and away from him on the next. Melvin caught the cue: he rocked forward when Lenny leaned back, and rocked back when Lenny leaned in. They had come up with their own spontaneous dance moves.

At the end, they bowed in unison to the applause of those in the room. They had done it! Dean Dougherty was smiling at them. They grabbed their instrument cases and followed the stagehand out to the hall. Melvin exhaled.

"We were smokin'!" Lenny said.

Melvin nodded. He sat in a chair against the wall and put his accordion away.

Lenny paced. "This is just the beginning—just the beginning!" He rubbed his hands together. Was he talking to himself or to Melvin? "I'm telling you, Mel, I can see us onstage in Seattle. Mr. Gene has connections to clubs there. After that, who knows? Los Angeles, maybe. But we won't stop there. We're going all the way to New York City and *Birdland*!"

Melvin didn't say anything. Who was he to squash Lenny's dreams? Fantasies, really, because Melvin knew he was never going to play accordion on a stage in Seattle, let alone New York. His dream was much simpler: to be able to open his mouth and have the sounds flow out, smooth and easy, like Lenny's playing. Like speaking was for every other person he had ever known.

Eventually, the man with the clipboard came through the door and invited them all back into the studio. Mr. Byrd got everyone's attention. "Thank you, everyone, for attending today's audition. We can only take eight acts each week, which is less than half of you. But remember you can come back anytime and try again—maybe after you've practiced for another month . . . or two." Had he glanced at Melvin?

Melvin was sure he had, sure their names would *not* be called, which he'd decided was just fine. He wasn't ready to be on television, even if the audience was only the small city of Spokane. That was still thousands of people!

"The Swingin' Saxoccordions . . ."

Melvin snapped to attention. Lenny gripped him by the shoulder. "We did it! We're in the show!" he whispered.

Melvin stared at the big gold star on the backdrop, dazed by the announcement. There was no turning back now.

CHAPTER TWENTY-ONE

'm telling you, it was beshert." Lenny bounced down the Boone Avenue sidewalk as if the concrete were a trampoline.

Melvin was excited too, but he was facing the reality that he would have to speak on television to thousands of viewers, and he really didn't see how he could. He would make a fool of himself! "Buh-buh-*shirt?*"

"'Meant to be.' Ma says it's like destiny. Or Divine Providence. It's beshert we made it onto the show. I knew we would!"

They were headed to the Spokane Club to tell Grandma Robinson the good news. They had to be back in the studio by four, only a couple hours from then, not enough time to return home. The lady at the reception desk had allowed them to use the phone to call their parents.

Talking on a phone was hard enough. Talking on a phone with people listening in was even worse. Melvin had frozen up so badly Lenny'd had to take the receiver and tell Mrs. Robinson her own son had earned a spot on the show.

Lenny covered the mouthpiece. "She wants to know if you'd rather have them in the studio or watching on TV."

"Tuh-tuh-tuh-TELEVISION!" He had to shout to get the word out, but he also wanted to emphasize they should stay home. He didn't need his family there feeling sorry for him as he choked on his own words.

Walking along Boone, it occurred to him how amazing television was. By some miraculous transmission of wave particles through the atmosphere, his and Lenny's images would be in every Spokane home that tuned their televisions to channel 4 in a matter of hours.

This made him think about Uncle Melvin, whose *still* image had been in most Negro homes in Spokane for several years after he'd died. Back then, in 1941, the year Melvin had been born, there hadn't been TVs. Or at least very few. There also wasn't a bomb that could kill hundreds of thousands of people in less than a second.

Did it always work that way? Did scientific progress always come with some terrible cost? Did discoveries always advance life and destruction at the same time? He would have to ask Mr. Farber about this. And when he did, maybe he would ask about Mr. Farber's speech-pathologist wife, as well. That wouldn't do him any good with the challenge he faced right then, but still . . . maybe she could help him going forward. Trying to fix the Stutter on his own didn't seem to be working. At least not as well as he needed it to.

They stopped at the corner where the Spokane Club stood on a bluff, overlooking Peaceful Valley. "That's where my grandma was raised," Melvin said, pointing to the tiny house below, not far from the raging falls. Two of his great-aunts, Aunt Maddie and Aunt Mavis, Grandma's sisters, still lived there.

"How long ago did your family come here?" Lenny asked. They started walking down the hill behind the club.

"At least ffffifty years. My mmmmom and puh-pops were born here. Their puh-parents were the ones who came up from the South. Looking for uh . . . uh-opportunities."

"Did they find them?"

"That's a guh-good question," Melvin said, pulling open the basement door to the Spokane Club—the servants' entrance.

They found Grandma in the kitchen pouring a light pink substance into a strange-looking round pan. She lit up when she saw Melvin, wiped her hands on her white apron, and came over immediately to squeeze him, as if she were making fresh orange juice.

"Well?" She looked into his eyes expectantly.

"Wwwe muh-made it," Melvin said, feeling his nervousness like a hummingbird in his chest.

She squeezed his cheeks, going for every last drop of juice. "Well, that's mighty marvelous! Just like you!"

Mighty Marvelous Melvin. Hmmm . . . he liked the sound of that. If he needed to have a stage name, as Lenny insisted, that wouldn't be a half-bad one. Except that it was more *M*'s for him to pronounce. Strike that.

"And you must be the Lenny my Melvin's been talking about."

All Lenny could get out was, "Yes, m—" before Grandma had scooped him into an embrace. His face would have landed smack-dab in her bosom, as squishy as the cinnamon rolls she was famous for, if he hadn't turned his head as quickly as he did.

Melvin cracked up at the surprised expression on Lenny's face. He'd never seen his friend look so caught off guard.

"Well, congratulations!" she said, releasing Lenny. "This calls for something special. We just won't tell Mr. Swanson." They followed her all the way in. The other employees ignored them. Grandma was the most senior kitchen employee and could do anything she wanted, including entertain guests.

"What *is* that?" Melvin peered at the chunky, pinkish substance in the pan. It reminded him of the time he'd gotten sick in the car on their way home from Curlew Lake.

"A molded salmon salad."

"Moldy?" Melvin asked, thinking of fuzzy stuff growing on rotten food.

"Not moldy. Molded. As in formed into a shape." She chuckled. "But I one hundred percent agree with the look on your face. These fancy white folks have the strangest ideas about what constitutes good food."

They toasted to that, and to Melvin and Lenny's imminent appearance on *Starlit Stairway*, with glasses of ginger ale. Then Grandma had an idea. "Let's go tell Mr. Swanson about you making it onto the show. Maybe he'll give me a short break and I can watch you on the television in his office."

A television in his office! Now that was a sign of true success.

They took the stairs to the ground level, and waited in front of the lobby elevator to take it to the top floor, where Mr. Swanson's office was located. While they were standing there, three white men in suits and ties walked up. One of them, who wore an engraved name badge on his lapel, narrowed his eyes at Grandma. "Gal, what are you doing out of the kitchen?"

"My grandson and his friend here, they just made it onto *Starlit Stairway*, and I am going upstairs to share the news with Mr. Swanson—sir." The title seemed like an afterthought.

The man with the badge scowled. "I'm showing two of our new members around. Head on back to your station, now." The elevator doors opened, and he beckoned for the two men to go first. Having dismissed Grandma, he followed them on, talking about the "privileges of club membership."

The elevator doors closed.

Grandma *humph*ed. "Well, I don't know who he thinks *he* is," she muttered. "Never mind him. How 'bout we get you some fancy club food for lunch?" She elbowed Melvin. "No moldy salmon salad, though. That's for dinner." Her brown eyes twinkled, and Melvin smiled, in spite of the bad taste that man had left in his mouth.

He and Lenny sat at the end of a long metal table in the kitchen and ate, doing their best to stay out of the way. After that, they ran the giant dishwasher a few times to give Old Bart a break. Old Bart had been running that dishwasher for at least fifteen years and had taught Melvin how to do it one summer about five years before.

Then, just like that, it was time to go back.

But first, Grandma had some words for Melvin. She planted herself in front of him. "Stand up, now."

He was afraid to look into his grandma's eyes.

She took his hands and waited for him to meet her gaze. "Now you listen here, Melvin Robinson. Don't you worry one little bit about them tricky words. Stuttering don't have to stop you from saying what you *got* to say. You hear me?"

He nodded, but his grandmother didn't know. It had stopped him, plenty of times.

She hugged him, and everyone in the kitchen sent them off with cries of "Good luck!" and one person shouted, "Break a leg!" which was a very odd way to wish someone well, Melvin thought. His goal was to get in and out of that soundstage without breaking *anything*—especially his pride.

CHAPTER TWENTY-TWO

t the studio, the receptionist admitted them and handed them a card marked with the number six, their order in the lineup. "My lucky number," Lenny said, grinning. The atmosphere was much more charged than it had been earlier. TV station people hustled and bustled up and down the hall and in and out of the studio.

They changed quickly in the dressing room. Melvin wrestled with his tie—how did Pops make it look so easy?—all the while talking to himself. You can do this. Just pretend you're jamming at Lenny's place, same as always.

But what about when Dean Dougherty started to interview them?

Lenny. Lenny loved to talk. Lenny could do all the talking!

How had he not thought of it already? He glanced at his friend, slicking his hair to the side in the mirror.

Suddenly, Grandma was in his ear, speaking to him again. *Stuttering don't have to stop you from saying what you got to say.*

Had she put emphasis on the word *got*, as he seemed to recall? *Stuttering don't have to stop you from saying what you* got *to say.* As in what he *must* say. What *he* must say.

What if he *had* to do this? Not for others, but for himself?

You must do the thing you think you cannot do. It was something Mom sometimes said. A quote from Mrs. Eleanor Roosevelt, the former First Lady.

Can't go through the rest of your life avoiding situations that require you to talk, he could hear Grandma Robinson saying. *Got to be able to talk to people in all those places you plannin' to travel to!*

Okay, he wouldn't ask Lenny to do all the talking. But if he was going to talk for himself . . . The panicky feeling started to rise.

He needed a plan. He would keep his words to a minimum. As usual, he would do his best to avoid all sticky letters. "Cleveland" was a hard stop; Lenny could answer the "What school do you attend?" question. "How long have you been playing accordion?" shouldn't be too bad. He'd just ease out the *F* on "four years" and let it ride on his breath. And as for what he wanted to be when he grew up—which Dean Dougherty always asked kids on the show—he honestly didn't know. Plus, he couldn't stand the question. A shoulder shrug for that one, and it would be over.

"Ten minutes 'til showtime!" someone called from the hall.

Melvin's fingers shook as he tried again to center the knot of his tie. It was as good as it was going to get. And so was his speaking. So he might as well just go out there and play.

In the hallway, they lined up by their numbers. Lenny chatted with act number five, the brother-sister performers. It turned out the balls and bowling pins were for juggling. Melvin felt like his accordion: tight and folded up. He hoped he would be able to loosen up again, as he had during the audition.

He leaned against the wall and did some tongue push-ups. The nice thing about Mr. Feuchtinger's method was that elements could be practiced anywhere, at any time, and no one would even know all the calisthenics going on inside his mouth.

The boy with the mouse got in line behind him.

Should he try to talk to him? Maybe it would help him relax. "Hhhhi," he started. Heat prickled in his armpits.

"Hi," the boy said back. "That looks like a hard instrument." He glanced at the accordion.

"It's nnnnnot so buh-buh—" Come on. Cooperate! He jerked his head. "Bad."

"Nervous?"

Did the boy think his stammer was only due to nerves? Nerves certainly weren't helping. He nodded. Of course he was nervous! They were about to appear on TV!

"I'm Andrew." The boy held out his hand. Melvin shook it. "And this is Squeakers." He lifted the cage. The little brown mouse huddled in a corner. Melvin knew how Squeakers felt.

"Mmmy nuh-name is Mmmmelvin."

George, the man with the clipboard, appeared from the soundstage. "Okay, attention, everyone!"

"Good luck, Melvin," Andrew whispered.

He wanted to tell Andrew that if he had to bet on who would win the twenty-five-dollar prize it would be him and Squeakers, but that was too many words to get out now. Plus, George was explaining how it was all going to work. They'd be standing in order "in the wings" (to the side of the stage behind the curtains) and needed to be very quiet. When announced, they were to enter the stage area, talk to Dean Dougherty for a moment, and then begin their act as quickly as possible. When they finished, they were to bow and return offstage so they could watch the show and wait for the winners to be announced.

"Got it?" George asked.

Melvin's brain felt like it was shorting out. He'd just follow Lenny.

Two girls wearing matching red sweaters and wavy, calf-length black skirts appeared. Everyone whispered in excitement. Lenny nudged him with his elbow. Melvin gulped. *The Boyle Fuel Twins!* They were the famous girls who sang the "Boyle Fuel" song at the beginning of every show, as well as other jingles in the middle and at the end. They looked about Maisy's age, seventh grade.

The twins wished everyone luck and disappeared into the studio. Next, it was the performers' turn. The line started to move.

"Here we go!" Lenny said.

Melvin's heart rate notched up. The stage was brightly lit. The wings were pitch dark. He heard people murmuring in the studio audience and imagined the Thirteen Black Cats and Mrs. Carini sitting out there, waiting for Lenny and him to appear. When Lenny had called home, he'd asked them all to come.

Melvin imagined his family gathered around their small TV— Mom, Pops, Marian, Maisy, Chuck. Would Chuck be watching? He'd played in a game earlier that day. Cleveland's team was on a four-game winning streak. Then Melvin thought of Millie, and suddenly he couldn't breathe. He pulled at his tie. He was messing up the knot, but . . . he couldn't breathe! Sweat beaded on his forehead and upper lip. Was he having a heart attack?

He grabbed Lenny's arm, starting to hyperventilate. "I duh-duh-don't thhhhh-think—"

"Melvin." Lenny's firm voice stopped Melvin's heart palpitations in their tracks. "We're doing this." His usual, upbeat tone returned. "And it's going to be great!"

Melvin took deep breaths, trying to calm himself the way Mr. Feuchtinger encouraged.

Dean Dougherty came through in a flurry of plaid, wishing them all luck (so many people were wishing them luck—but Melvin didn't mind, he needed it), and then George shouted from the stage, "Quiet on the set!"

Melvin could hear the tiny claws of Squeakers the mouse scrabbling around next to him.

The twins had gotten into position in front of the bright yellow backdrop. Then George said loudly, "In five, four, three, two—"

A voice Melvin recognized from TV announced: "It's time for . . . *Starlit Stairway!*"

The sisters began to sing:

When you need coal or oil, call Boyle

Fairfax 8-1521

Fairfax 8-1521

For every heating problem,

Be your furnace old or new,

Just call the Boyle Fuel Company,

And they'll solve them all for you!

Dean Dougherty jogged onto the stage from the other side. The audience cheered. "Good evening, viewers! Tonight promises to be another sizzling half hour of entertainment provided by our own highly talented local youth!"

More cheering and clapping. A high-pitched whistle from the audience caused Lenny to lean in. "I bet that was Gene," he whispered. The Thirteen Black Cats' bandleader. Melvin's heart thumped hard again.

"The eight acts that cut the mustard earlier today are all fantastic in their own way, but we will be singling out three that the judges feel merit special recognition. And, as usual, our grand prize winner will receive the *twenty-five-dollar* prize!"

The audience responded with an enthusiastic round of applause. Even in the dark, Melvin could see Lenny's gleaming teeth. Melvin was too scared to smile. He hugged his accordion and tried to keep his breathing as steady as possible.

The first act went off without a hitch. The whole time, Melvin did his tongue push-ups like crazy. He kept wiping his sweaty palms on his pants. He couldn't hold his accordion firmly with sweating palms!

Two more acts, and then the Boyle Fuel Twins sang their commercial ditty about Caterized Oil.

By the fourth act, a Hula-Hooping girl duo, Melvin actually felt himself relaxing. Everything was going along fine. He and Lenny would be fine. *He* would be fine.

When the brother-and-sister jugglers got onstage, however, the boy, who was probably no older than seven, stared blankly into the audience. "Mother, I have to use the toilet," he said plainly. He crossed his legs.

There were some twitters and chuckles from the audience, as George hissed from nearby, "Hey, kid with the accordion! You and your buddy are up!"

Melvin jumped. What? Now?

Dean Dougherty hurried onto the stage and ushered the boy into George's arms. "That's all right, young man, I remember when I was first starting out . . . nerves most certainly can cause the *urge* to kick in." George led the boy and his sister offstage.

"We'll get them back, ladies and gentlemen, uh, after business has been taken care of. In the meantime, let's welcome onto the Starlit Stairway stage"—he read from the card in his hand—"Melvin Robinson and Lenny 'Crazy Man' Carini, the Swingin' Saxoccordions!"

It all happened so fast Melvin didn't have time to think. He simply followed Lenny onto the set and stood there next to Dean Dougherty. His tongue felt as dry as the venison jerky Pops made one deer-hunting season.

"So, you young men are freshmen at Cleveland High School, is that correct?"

"That's right. Go Tigers!" Lenny said, looking into the camera.

"And, 'Crazy Man,' why that stage name?"

Lenny grinned at Melvin. "*He* gave it to me. 'Cuz he said I was crazy if I thought I could get him to try out for *Starlit Stairway*."

Dean Dougherty chuckled, looking at Melvin. "And here you are! Not so crazy after all, huh?"

Lenny jumped in. "I blow my *horn* like crazy!" People laughed. He made it seem so easy.

"And, Melvin . . ." Dean Dougherty looked at his paper. "How about you? How long have you been playing accordion?"

It was the question Melvin had hoped he'd get.

He took a breath. Nice and easy. No forcing—

Frozen.

Everything.

Lips, tongue, vocal cords, diaphragm. All of it!

He tried again to speak.

Blocked.

He was sweating under the lights. Too much time was passing! He was pushing so hard to get a word—*any* word—out, his eyeballs felt like they might pop right out of their sockets.

A sharp rap against his back sent the words shooting like bullets from Pops's rifle: "Fouryearssir!"

Dean Dougherty had slapped him! Even more amazing, it had worked!

The host's smile hadn't changed the whole time, but his eyes showed his bewilderment. "Well, uh . . . Wow! That's some dedication right there. Okay, enough talk. Let's hear some music!" He was back to his slick, TV-host self. "Ladies and gentlemen, I give you . . . the Swingin' Saxoccordians!" He backed offstage, arms extended toward Melvin and Lenny.

Melvin got his accordion into position. He felt shaky, but relieved too. He had blocked—bad—and he'd also survived.

But Millie! He could practically feel her pity coming at him through the cameras.

Lenny caught his eye. "Ready?" he whispered.

Melvin didn't want anyone's pity. He wanted to be mighty. He would go to war with the Stutter, and he *would* win!

He gave a quick nod. Lenny counted off. And like that, they were playing.

Melvin channeled all eight years of frustration over his broken tongue into his arms. He played so furiously it took him a few moments to look up and realize Lenny was doing the back-and-forth motion with his body. Melvin joined in and they rocked in time to the music they were making.

When he felt his voice bubbling up, he decided he wouldn't stop it. His voice wanted to come out; he opened his lips and let it. "It makes no difference if that tune is sweet or hot, just give that rhythm . . . everything you got!"

Sweet as Nat King Cole. Hot as Chuck Berry. He hoped Miss Gale was watching! He *knew* Millie was. The thought made his heart soar and he sang some more. Smooth as honey.

They jammed together, in perfect sync. Melvin could *feel* the electricity as if currents passed between him and Lenny and them and the audience. He heard someone holler, "That's right boys, give it all you got!" *Miss Inez.* Melvin would recognize the Harlem Club singer's husky voice anywhere.

Beads of perspiration trickled down the sides of his face. Between the stage lights and his vigorous playing, he was working up a sweat. And it was no longer a nervous one.

When they finished, the applause was loud. Melvin heard whistles and whoops, most likely from members of the Thirteen Black Cats.

He was pretty sure his own grin was big enough to mirror Lenny's. The thoughts passing between them were nearly audible.

You did it. We did it. You sang! I sang!!!

Dean Dougherty came back onstage as Melvin and Lenny hustled off. "You were smokin'!" Lenny whispered. "Did you know you were going to sing?"

"No, it just happened. Hope you don't mind."

"Are you kidding? It was fantastic!"

Melvin couldn't sit down. His nerves were still abuzz. The tremor in his fingers had worked itself all the way up his arms. They were vibrating. His throat and mouth felt open and free and full of energy, like he could talk all night long. He had never felt so alive!

While he tried to calm himself down, Andrew was onstage with Squeakers, doing his routine. Audience laughter punctuated the act. Clapping signaled they were done, and Andrew returned behind the curtain, holding Squeakers to his chest. He set the cage down. "Phew, glad that's over! How about you, Squeaks? Were you scared?" He held the mouse in his cupped palms, stroking its fur.

"Great job," Melvin whispered. It was as if the Stutter had been routed by Melvin's triumphant performance and had retreated to an unknown location. Melvin hadn't felt this confident . . . well, maybe ever.

After one more performance, and the do-over for the brother-sister performers, the Boyle Fuel Twins sang their last ditty. Then it was time to announce the winners.

"Well, folks, I told you we had an incredible show for you! Was I right?" Dean Dougherty grinned at the camera. "The judges were exceptionally challenged tonight, but choose they must and so . . ."

He held a paper up in front of him. Lenny nudged Melvin, his eyes wide with anticipation.

"Third place goes to Ann Poppenroth!" The girl who'd tap-danced while playing piano shrieked and click-clacked onto the set.

"Second place goes to Andrew Simpkins—and Squeakers, his mouse!"

"Good job!" Melvin patted the boy on the back, who stood and walked onstage, carrying Squeakers in his cage.

Melvin had predicted two of the three winners. Maybe he should become a gambling man. It was a bit disappointing not to have won a runner-up prize, as he felt sure their performance had deserved at least that much.

"And the winner is . . . the *Swingin' Saxoccordions!*"

Melvin was being pulled from his chair. Lenny had grabbed him and run. The Thirteen Black Cats thundered and cheered. Melvin took Lenny's outstretched hand, and they bowed again and again.

Marvelous. Melodious. Mighty. Melvin felt all of that and more. And he didn't have to talk about any of it. He just was.

No words needed.

CHAPTER TWENTY-THREE

Melvin's family was ecstatic about his and Lenny's first-place performance, especially Mom, who said more than once after she picked Melvin up from the studio, "I always *knew* that accordion would get you on TV!"

Even Chuck was enthusiastic. He threw his arm around Melvin's neck and scrubbed his head affectionately. "What are you going to do with your half of the prize money?"

Melvin shrugged, even though he knew. *Hammond's New Supreme Atlas*. So he could hold the world in his hands.

* * *

At school on Monday, Melvin and Lenny were practically celebrities. It seemed as if everyone had seen the show. In homeroom they got a round of applause, except from Gary and Troy, who sat stonily, their faces impassive.

When class ended, kids surrounded their desks, wanting to know what it was like to be on TV. Lenny answered their questions, while Melvin watched Millie. She was still at her desk, putting her books in her bag. When she looked over at him and smiled, he felt himself light up. He grinned in return. She left the room, but he knew: she was happy for him.

Mr. Farber had a special experiment that day, in honor of "their *Starlit Stairway* champions"—a demonstration on sound waves.

In choir, Miss Gale gave him high praise for his singing and playing.

"How did it feel to perform on TV?" Warren Hashbrook asked. As a male tenor, Melvin sat smack-dab in the middle of the four curved rows of kids all wanting to know the same. He started to sweat. Lenny wasn't there to talk for him this time.

"It wwwwwas a—" The invisible lid slammed down on his larynx.

The whole choir watched. Waited.

He opened his mouth again, but this time he sang: "It was aaaaaa-maaaaaa-zing!"

Kids laughed and nodded their approval. He smiled and joined them. Then Miss Gale started playing the piano and everyone sang together.

All morning, Melvin waited for Gary to give him grief, but for once it seemed Gary was the one who couldn't find words. He didn't even look at Melvin when they passed in the hall.

At lunch, it was hard not to notice kids staring, nudging each other and whispering, as he and Lenny passed by. Some pointed. Melvin scanned the cafeteria for the one person he wanted to see: Millie. Lenny, who always brought food from the Harlem Club (lucky him!), found them seats while Melvin headed for the hot-food line. If Millie was there, he couldn't find her.

He grabbed a tray and put it on the metal bars that ran alongside the food offerings like train tracks. The air smelled like a mix of that day's main course options: crispy, golden corn dogs, and meatloaf, his absolute *least* favorite.

He looked for "his" lunch lady—the nice one who had figured out that he preferred to point to his choices. Apparently, she wasn't serving food that day. His eyes searched the kitchen, but she wasn't there either. In her place was an older white woman with clipped speech and an impatient air. Frown lines framed her tensed mouth like parentheses and etched the space between her eyes like quotation marks.

He repeated in his head: Corn dog . . . corn dog . . . c-o-o-orn dog. Smooth and steady, like the lunch trays going down the track. He'd been having a great day—not because he hadn't stuttered, but because it didn't seem to matter so much. Still, he didn't want that hard *C* to trip him up!

The closer he got to the lady with her hair looking like a silver fish in a net, the more he could feel the tension building. A steel band constricted his chest. A hand was around his throat. He stood in front of her and pointed, hoping she might understand.

"Don't you point and expect me to obey. You ask politely, young man."

His tongue felt as if it had swelled up to twice its size.

CORN DOG! his thoughts screamed. His eyes darted about, looking for a friend to help him out. Gary stood a few kids down the line, smirking. "What's wrong, Skip? Cat got your tongue?"

A red-headed boy behind Melvin whispered, "You want the corn dog?"

Melvin nodded quickly. But the woman, who clearly had the patience of a gnat, said, "We gotta keep things moving," and handed him the meatloaf.

"He wanted the corn dog," the boy said, but Melvin took the plate and shuffled forward.

"Well, then, next time he can say so," the lady said.

Someone bumped Melvin from behind, almost causing him to drop his tray. "Guess being a TV star doesn't make you any less of a broken record," Gary snarled.

Melvin glared at Gary's back as he strutted away. Gary was bigger than Melvin, by at least fifty pounds and six inches, but in his mind, Melvin could take him down. He imagined himself leaping on Gary, knocking him to the ground, and pounding him with his fists until the goon was beaten into submission.

"Bullies are actually very small people." Millie stood beside him, tray in hand. She wore a pink dress and a string of pearls. Her hair was neatly pinned up. It swept across her forehead in a way that reminded him of an ocean wave.

He hoped she hadn't heard what Gary said.

"Never mind him. You were incredible, Melvin." Her onyx eyes shone. He loved their graceful shape, how they stood out so clearly on her face.

"Thank . . . you." He looked down at his tray. "Do you wwwwant to eat with us?" He glanced toward where Lenny had sat.

"I would, but some friends are waiting for me. I just wanted you to know . . . you were marvelous." There was that word again. *Marvelous.* It sounded amazing coming from Millie's lips. She smiled; then she turned and walked away.

He wanted to call after her—to tell her he'd been planning to ask her to Homecoming, that she was the only one he really wanted to go with. But, of course, he wasn't going to do that. Not here, not now. Probably not ever.

Melvin stared at the mushy meatloaf on his tray. He tried to hear only Millie's words, but Gary's taunts were tromping all over them. Who was he kidding? He wasn't a TV star. He was back to being a sideshow spectacle.

CHAPTER TWENTY-FOUR

With three of them getting ready for the Homecoming Dance, the Robinson household was abuzz. Melvin had been told not to come to the back of the house, where Marian was at the center of some kind of mysterious preparation ceremony. He was happy to stay away. Acrid smells—the pressing iron's hot metal, burning hair, and that fumy hair spray—had overtaken everything. In the bathroom, it was the pungent aromas of Chuck's aftershave and medicinal mouthwash. Their bedroom was the only safe place to be, and there Melvin dressed, reluctantly.

"I can't believe I have to do this, Tuck," he said, buttoning up his shirt. "This is *horrible*. No one asked me if I wanted to go with Eugenia—or if I even wanted to *go*. Not my fault white boys don't ask Negro girls to dances." What would happen if one of them did? he wondered. Probably all heck would break loose. It was another line people knew not to cross.

"Melvin! You getting ready in there?" Mom's nervous energy was enough to light up the entire block.

"Yes."

"Good. It's about time for a picture!" Thankfully, she didn't feel the need to enter the room and do a whole bunch of fussing over him too. For the past twenty-four hours she'd been waiting on Marian hand and foot as if the queenship had already been bestowed. They would know later that evening if Marian had won the crown.

Melvin brought his tie to the living room, where Pops and Maisy played cribbage on the side table next to the recliner. Maisy had made it clear she was absolutely *not* feeling envious or left out in any way, but she still looked pouty.

"Too bad you're going to miss *Starlit Stairway* tonight," Maisy said. "Especially after your big win last week."

"Buh-believe me, I'd—rather be sssstaying home with you than going to this dumb *dance*." Melvin stood face-to-face with Pops, who had finished cinching the tie around Melvin's neck.

Pops chuckled. "Don't let your mother hear you say that." He thumped Melvin on the back. "Lookin' mighty dapper, son. Gonna have yourself a night to remember, for sure."

A night to forget was more like it. What was Millie doing at that moment? Had anyone asked her to the dance? The thought of seeing her there with someone else made his chest hurt.

Clomping footsteps on the front porch gave away Bubba and Mr. Jessup. They practically had to duck to get inside the Robinsons' house.

Mom bustled into the living room. "Oh, Francis! Don't you look handsome?"

"Thank you, Mrs. Robinson," Bubba said politely.

Bubba's hair was greased smooth and flat, with an off-center part. He carried a plastic container that held a corsage of white flowers that looked carved out of Ivory soap. His lips barely concealed a smile as he spied the fuchsia boutonniere on Melvin's jacket. Bubba wore a royal-blue silk kerchief in his breast pocket. No flowers. Melvin dared him with his eyes to say something about the boutonniere. He would let Bubba have it about his playboy handkerchief.

"Thanks for letting him ride with your boys," Mr. Jessup said. "See you at the track tomorrow, Claude?"

Mom's eyes slid to meet Pops's. "On a Sunday?"

"There's plenty of time in the day for church *and* leisure," Pops said.

"But it's the Lord's Day."

"On which the Lord commanded us to rest, and watching horses run at Playfair sure seems restful to *me*."

Mr. Jessup cleared his throat. "Well, you just let me know. Son, have a great time, and don't do anything I wouldn't do!" He patted Bubba's shoulder and left.

Mom disappeared into the back.

Bubba came to the other side of the television so he wasn't blocking anyone's view. "You ready for this?" he said under his breath.

Melvin simply gave him a sideways look. What do you think? he made his face say. He clutched his stomach and was considering dropping to the ground as if overtaken by some kind of horrible pangs when Chuck made a sound like a trumpet fanfare from the kitchen.

"Announcing the next Grover Cleveland High School Homecoming Queen . . . Marian Esther Hermia Robinson!"

Chuck and Marian appeared arm in arm in the doorway. Marian's dress was cream-colored satin. She wore fancy, long white gloves and her Homecoming Princess sash. Pearl-and-crystal earrings dangled from her earlobes.

She looked like a *real* princess. Melvin dropped his arms to his sides, silenced. Maisy gasped and jumped up to hug her. Bubba muttered, "Wow."

Pops quoted one of his poets: "A thing of beauty is a joy for ever: Its loveliness increases; it will never pass into nothingness . . ."

Melvin would go to the dance—for his sister. "You llllook buh- . . . really nuh-nice." *Beautiful* was too flowery anyway.

Marian smiled regally. Then she looked down at her feet, seeming suddenly bashful. "Thank you."

Pops took her hand and spun her into the center of the room, where everyone posed for too many pictures. (Melvin feared he wouldn't regain his sight after all the camera flashes.) Then it was time to go, and Melvin was swept along in the current of the most important Homecoming ever in the history of Spokane.

* * *

On the way to the Purcells' Melvin asked Bubba how Franceda was, and did she mind he was taking another girl to the dance?

"Nah, man. She ended it anyway. Said she was too busy to keep writing."

Melvin scrunched his face to communicate that was tough luck, but Bubba just shrugged. "Hey, we're young, right? Lots of time to find the right one."

Melvin had never told Bubba anything about his feelings toward Millie. He didn't know if or when he would. He kind of liked having it just to himself. His own sacred secret.

They pulled up outside the Purcells'. Melvin watched Bubba closely from the car so he would know what to do when it was his turn. Bubba walked up the front steps, holding his little plastic container of flowers, rang the doorbell, and disappeared inside. Sylvia appeared in the doorway a few minutes later, the flowers pinned near the neckline of her dress. Bubba quickly moved to her side and escorted her down the front steps.

Looked easy enough. Except for the disappearing inside part. Melvin really didn't want to have to make conversation with Mr. and Mrs. Dalbert. And also, the flowers. How had Bubba gotten them pinned to her chest? Melvin stared at the corsage Mom had handed him as he walked out the door. The task seemed more treacherous than fording a crocodile-infested river.

Sylvia and Bubba slid in beside Melvin. A thick smell of flowery perfume overtook him. His nose twitched and quivered. He sneezed. And again. And once more. His eyes watered. "Ah-choo!"

Marian turned in her seat. "Are you okay, Melvin?"

He nodded, trying not to breathe in too deeply because it made the tickle more intense, but he couldn't stop it. "Ah-choo. Ah-choo. Ahhhhh-chooooo!" Out of the corner of his eye, he could see Sylvia staring.

"What's wrong with him?" she asked.

Chuck eyed him in the rearview mirror.

I'm allergic to dances and setup dates, Melvin thought miserably.

Bubba nudged him with his elbow. He held out the royal-blue hankie.

Melvin tried to wave it away. He couldn't use *that* to blow his nose! Not the dandy handkerchief.

"You know I don't care," Bubba said. "I'm only wearing it because my mom made me. Take it."

Melvin reached for the silky square. He stared at it, waiting to see if his nose was done. It wasn't. He sneezed into it four more times.

"Maybe he's allergic to gardenias," Marian said. "That corsage looks really pretty with your dress."

Sylvia thanked her and suddenly the girls were chattering away, about Marian's dress fabric, and how she felt about Homecoming Queen, and who they were going to look for at the dance.

Glad to no longer be the focus of attention, Melvin wadded up the handkerchief and handed it back to Bubba, who looked at him like he was crazy.

"Just puh-playing," Melvin said. They laughed, while Sylvia looked on, clearly disgusted.

It felt good to laugh, and he suddenly wished Lenny was there with them. When the Thirteen Black Cats had found out Lenny didn't have a date for Homecoming, they'd taken pity on him and finally invited him to play with them. Of course, Melvin knew Lenny had no interest at all in going to the dance. He'd practically been levitating when he'd told Melvin the news. What Melvin wouldn't give to be there at the club instead of where he was! Even if it was a "whites only" night and he had to stand backstage.

They pulled up to the Dalberts'. Melvin sat there, clutching the plastic container of flowers he had no idea how to get on his date. Chuck turned in the driver's seat. "You trying to summon her by telepathy? Go get her already."

Melvin got out of the car. He moved forward slowly, like a new army recruit making his first foray into battle. Chuck should be the one taking Eugenia, he thought. They were much closer in age. Melvin could escort Marian. He almost turned around to suggest it, but the Dalberts' front door opened and Mrs. Dalbert called to him.

"Good evening, Melvin! Come now. Your lady awaits!"

His lady?

He glanced over his shoulder. Thankfully, he didn't think they could hear Mrs. Dalbert.

He walked up the front steps and into the house. Eugenia stood waiting in their small front room, wearing a dark-blue dress covered in sparkles. It reminded Melvin of the nighttime sky at Curlew Lake. A small pang of regret that he wasn't looking at Millie plucked his heart.

"You . . . you look vvvery nuh-nuh-nnnice?" His face burned. He hadn't stuttered once in the hundred times he'd practiced it on Tuck that day. And why had he said it like a question? Stupid!

"Thank you."

Mrs. Dalbert rushed forward, her hands outstretched. "What lovely flowers. Here, may I help?"

Melvin shoved the clear box into her hands, nodding eagerly. Mr. Dalbert stood nearby, arms folded across his chest, like a general sizing up a soldier. The man may have been smallish in stature, but he was making his fatherly protection known in a big way. Melvin's legs quaked.

Mr. Dalbert looked at Melvin with an eagle eye. "To the dance and home again."

Melvin wanted to say it wasn't really up to him, his brother was the one driving, but he knew better. Plus, he didn't plan to open his mouth again.

Eugenia piped up from behind her mother, who was still positioning the corsage. "Oh, Daddy. You don't need to be so stern. Melvin's doing us a favor, remember?"

The hard line of Mr. Dalbert's jaw softened a little. His eyes softened too, but he was looking at his daughter, not at Melvin. "He's the one who should be grateful—getting to go to Homecoming with the most beautiful gal at Cleveland High."

"Oh, Daddy. Stop."

Mrs. Dalbert stepped back and gave her daughter an approving nod.

Melvin stiffened his body, trying to stop the shaking. He *really* didn't want to have to speak again.

"Off you go, then. Your carriage awaits!" Mrs. Dalbert shooed them out the door, and just like that, Melvin was on his first official date.

CHAPTER TWENTY-FIVE

The street in front of the high school was crawling with cars looking for parking spots. Melvin had crammed into the far back of the station wagon rather than be too close to either girl, although he cited protecting their dresses from wrinkles as the reason. He looked out the rear window at couples walking toward the entrance.

He imagined Millie in a pink chiffon dress decorated with cherry blossoms just like the tree where he had first seen her, the summer before they started first grade. Millie had been sitting in the V where the cherry tree's trunk divided in two, partially hidden by the green leaves. Her family had been moving in. He'd watched from his porch. He suddenly remembered thinking at the time that it didn't seem like they had very much. Now he knew why. They'd been in that prison camp, and been forced to give up most of what they owned.

He glimpsed a pink dress between cars, and his breath caught in his throat. But the girl wearing it was a blonde, on the arm of a tall boy Melvin recognized as one of Chuck's teammates. Chuck parked and they all got out of the car, Melvin last because he had to wait for someone to open the back.

They walked toward the school as a group. He really hoped Bubba wouldn't hold out his arm for Sylvia to take. Then he would feel obliged to do the same for Eugenia. The sound of live music floated down the hall from the gym. Mr. Farber was taking tickets at the entrance. *How does he use his hook so dexterously?* Melvin wondered as they waited in line. His teacher never once hesitated or dropped a ticket. He smiled and made jokes. He seemed completely at ease.

"Ah, another of our Princesses has arrived," Mr. Farber said, taking the tickets from Chuck's hand. Marian beamed. "Along with her gallant escort. Super job on the field last night, by the way."

Chuck bowed his head. "Thank you, sir."

"Miss Dalbert, I see you have excellent taste. You're escorting one of my finest freshman students."

Chuck sucked in his lips. Apparently, he found the idea of Eugenia escorting Melvin (and not the other way around) funny.

"Not to mention he plays a mean accordion." Mr. Farber winked at Melvin. "Speaking of, where's your usual sidekick?"

"Hhhhe got his ffffirst official gig tonight—at the Harlem Cuh-Club."

Mr. Farber nodded, looking impressed. He greeted Sylvia and then smiled up at Bubba. "And who do we have escorting Miss Purcell tonight?"

"Bubba Jessup, sir." Bubba started to hold out his hand but pulled it back awkwardly when he saw Mr. Farber's hook.

"I know it looks lethal, but I promise I won't maul you. You should see the first few I practiced on, though." Mr. Farber shook his head, grimacing. "Got hooks of their own now."

Bubba returned Mr. Farber's smile and grasped his extended left hand.

"Pleasure, Bubba. Welcome to Cleveland. Now get on in there and have a great time! And good luck, Marian." He shielded his mouth with his hand but Melvin was close enough to hear him say, with a wink, "I hope you win tonight."

Melvin crossed the threshold into the gym-turned-jungle for the "Safari Soirée." The basketball hoops had been converted into palm trees covered in twinkling lights. Grass-hut roofs, also outlined in lights, had been constructed over long tables that held finger foods and punch. An area where couples got their picture taken included a complete grass hut and a painting of palm trees under a full moon. The band, similar in style to the Thirteen Black Cats, except with all white musicians, played on a constructed stage in front of a backdrop of a safari vehicle parked in front of a pride of lions.

Marian and Chuck found some friends and went to dance. Bubba gazed around the gym, wide-eyed. "At ours, there were some streamers on the walls and a few balloons. This is *crazy*."

Thankfully, Eugenia and Sylvia seemed happy to talk to each other. They sat at a table while Bubba and Melvin went to get food. Melvin felt like he could eat the entire tray of meatballs. As he filled his plate, he surveyed the room, looking for Millie. The longer he went without seeing her there, the better he felt.

He was feeling really good as he and Bubba went back for seconds a while later. He'd even gone out on the dance floor with Eugenia when the band had started up a catchy song with a chorus that repeated "ah-wimoweh" over and over.

Still no Millie. Perhaps she had stayed at home. His heart thrilled at the thought.

"Hey, Jungle Boy," he heard from behind. He didn't have to look to know it was Gary. "You must feel right at home, *Sambo*." He and Troy laughed their irritating, mocking laughter.

They stopped abruptly when Bubba stepped between them and Melvin. "I think I missed the joke."

Gary, even though he was taller than Melvin, still had to look up to meet Bubba's eyes. "Hey, it's cool. Melvin knows I'm just kidding. Right, Melvin?"

The girl on Gary's arm looked at Melvin with sudden interest. "Are you Chuck Robinson's brother?" she asked.

The band started up with one of the summer's biggest hits: "One, two, three o'clock, four o'clock rock . . ."

Gary's eyes narrowed. "Come on. I want to dance." Gary turned, pulling his date along. She glanced over her shoulder as she went, then disappeared with Gary into the crowd of dancers, twisting and spinning around the floor to "Rock Around the Clock."

"The Rat's still up to his same old sorry tricks, huh?"

Melvin nodded. Truth be told, Gary had actually gotten *worse* since they'd arrived at Cleveland.

"He's bad news," Bubba said, shaking his head.

Melvin didn't need anyone to tell *him* that. He munched on potato chips, glad to see Marian on the dance floor, laughing and having a good time. She deserved that much, no matter how the teachers, football team, and other seniors had voted.

The song ended and Gary and his date returned to a table. He actually pulled out the seat for her like a real gentleman before heading toward the exit. Probably going to the bathroom, Melvin thought. He fantasized about following him in there and beating him with his bare fists. Yeah, right. Like that was ever going to happen.

Gary's girl was staring at him. Melvin put his paper plate in the garbage can near the buffet and pulled on Bubba's sleeve. "Want to hit the buh-bathroom with me?" he said. Maybe between him and Bubba they could give Gary a scare, at least.

"Nah, I'm good," Bubba said.

"I've rrrrreally got to go," Melvin said.

Bubba shrugged and dumped his plate, and they headed in the direction of the door.

"Hey!" The girl had caught up to them. Her cheeks were flushed pink. "I'm Barbara. What's your name again? Nelson?"

He had to jerk his head to get the sound started. "Mmmmelvin."

She looked embarrassed, whether because she got his name wrong or he stuttered, he couldn't be sure. "Oh, right. So, I was wondering . . . do you think you could introduce me to your brother? This would be the perfect time."

You mean, because that brute you came with is out of the room? "Ummm, mmmaybe later. He's—uh . . ." Melvin searched the large, crowded gym for his brother's fade cut. Chuck was on the floor doing the Lindy Hop with Arnetta Carter.

The girl, Barbara, grabbed his arm. "Just tell him he has an admirer who wants to meet him. Will you?" Her starstruck eyes were wide with excitement.

Oh brother. "Yeah, sure."

Her gaze flicked toward the door; she pulled her hand away quickly. "Just maybe . . . when Gary's not around," she said, and rushed off. The Rat had sauntered back into the gym. His eyes were slits. He headed straight for Melvin.

Thankfully, Principal Brill had taken the stage and was inviting the royal court to come forward. Melvin joined the throng of kids pressing in to hear the Homecoming Queen announced, glad for the protection of the crowd.

"Do you see Marian?" Eugenia asked. She and Sylvia had found their way to Melvin and Bubba. Eugenia stood on her toes trying to locate the royal court.

Melvin pointed. Chuck and Marian stood together in a line with the other Princesses and their dates. They walked up steps that led to the stage and assembled in a row behind Principal Brill.

The crowd cheered as Principal Brill announced each Princess. When Marian's name was called, Melvin, Bubba, Eugenia, and Sylvia whooped loudly. Melvin's chest swirled with pride. The whole thing had seemed silly initially, but now that the moment was here, he really wanted his sister to win. Plus, now he understood: this would be a big victory for them all.

The principal pulled a slip of paper from his breast pocket. He unfolded it—rather slowly, Melvin thought with impatience—and cleared his throat. "And the Cleveland High Homecoming Queen for 1955 is . . ."

A drumroll sounded from behind the principal.

"Lauren Hatmaker!"

The drummer hit a cymbal, and everyone cheered again. Except for Melvin, and the three people standing nearest him.

The band played while Lauren Hatmaker was crowned with a sparkly tiara. A female teacher helped replace the girl's Princess sash with one that said "Homecoming Queen." Marian looked on, applauding politely. She was smiling, but what was going on in her mind? It dawned on Melvin that it would be one thing for Marian to be disappointed for herself. It was a whole other thing when the hopes of an entire community were riding on your shoulders. He wanted to run up and throw his arms around her, just as she had when he'd come home from his and Lenny's win on *Starlit Stairway*.

The band started up another song, a *slow* one: "Ohhhhh, my love, my darling, I've hungered for your touch." *Yuck*. Melvin needed to get out of there—and *quick*. Thankfully, Eugenia was caught up in talking to Sylvia about the outcome of the contest. Melvin searched for an escape route through the crowded dance floor. Embracing couples swayed and shuffled around him and Bubba.

Suddenly, people were moving away. Gary, Troy, Larry Schmidt, and a couple other white boys formed a semicircle around Melvin like a mini-battalion.

"Why were you talking to my girlfriend?" Gary growled. "You think you're good enough for her?"

Melvin's eyes bounced from one stony face to the next. These white boys were serious.

"She came up to him," Bubba interjected. "Why don't you go ask her?"

Barbara was nowhere in sight.

"I don't care. What I *saw* was you talking to my date. So maybe she doesn't know what's good for her. But neither do you."

Melvin was sweating bad. His mind had gone blank. Even if he'd had a good comeback, he couldn't have gotten it out of his cotton-dry mouth.

"Leave him alone," Bubba said forcefully. "If you know what's good for *you*." Sylvia was pulling on his arm, whispering something about not getting involved. Eugenia seemed to have disappeared.

Gary laughed. "That's rich. You want to take us on? Come on, then. Got five on two. You don't stand a chance. Just like your sister. I mean, really, a Negro—as Homecoming Queen?"

You can't let him talk about Marian like that! Melvin thought as he glanced around, looking for Chuck.

Bubba growled. "What did you just say?"

"What's going on here?" Mr. Farber pushed his way into the circle. Eugenia was back. She glared fiercely at Gary. Chuck and Marian appeared, as well, their faces creased with concern.

"Nothing, Mr. Farber." Gary smiled.

What a liar!

"Just a little friendly banter. No harm done."

No harm done to *him*. But if Melvin had his way . . .

"Let's keep it that way. Break it up."

Gary's jaw bulged. Melvin felt kids staring, curious about what was going on. Gary motioned to the others and they walked away.

"You all right, gentlemen?" Mr. Farber asked.

Melvin nodded, although he was raging inside. His ears rang so loudly he couldn't think. He swallowed, trying to get his mouth to unclench.

"Well, if they give you any more trouble, be sure to let me know. Okay? You did the right thing getting me, Eugenia."

They all nodded, and Mr. Farber went back to patrolling the dance floor. He used his hook to tap on the shoulder of a boy whose mouth was getting a little too close to his date's.

Chuck put his hand on Melvin's shoulder. "You all right?"

Melvin's limbs buzzed and his face tingled. His heart thumped irregularly. He had been an antelope surrounded by lions there in the "jungle" of the gym. He was still mad at his brother for turning a blind eye the last time Gary'd had him cornered.

"Sure," he muttered. He turned and looked at Marian. "I'm ssssssorry you didn't . . . you didn't wwwwwin."

She shrugged. "It's okay."

"Being a Princess is still a big deal," Eugenia offered. Marian smiled.

"What do you say we jet?" Chuck asked.

They all agreed. The Homecoming Dance was no longer the place to be. Not for them, anyway.

Melvin knew exactly where he *did* want to be. At the Harlem Club, watching his "dish of milk" friend play saxophone with thirteen black cats.

CHAPTER TWENTY-SIX

I bet the Galaxy will be hoppin'," Chuck said as they walked through the parking lot, looking for Big Bertha.

The Galaxy was a hangout spot just for them—created by some businessmen in the Negro community who wanted a safe place for their young people to be able to have some food and fun. There was always music and dancing. Chuck went there regularly, but Melvin had only been once. Chuck hadn't exactly jumped at the chance to take him either. Mom had made Chuck bring him along.

Melvin tried to sound nonchalant. "Wwwwhat about the Hhhharlem Cuh-Club? Lenny's playing."

Chuck shot him a look. "Last time I checked, that place was 'whites only' on Saturdays. Unless you plan for us to sneak in as waiters?"

"Lenny lives there. Hhhhe can get us in." He talked confidently, even though he didn't actually know for certain. If it had been just him, yes. But six of them?

"Your new friend lives at the Harlem Club?" Bubba's eyebrows lifted. "You never told me *that*."

"You know Mom and Dad wouldn't approve of us going there," Marian said.

"Neither would my parents," Sylvia said. "You can take me home."

Melvin looked at Bubba, who shrugged. "Sure, I'll go."

"Me too," Eugenia said, to Melvin's surprise. "It's a dumb policy, anyway," she added. "And about time someone challenged it. It'll be our own little protest."

They reached the car and Chuck unlocked the passenger door to let Marian in. "What do you think?" he asked her.

"Well . . . I do agree with Eugenia. It is a dumb policy. And the fact that I couldn't ride the elevator at the Davenport . . ." Marian huffed. "That still gets my goat. So, yes. Let's do it."

Even though Melvin agreed with his sister, it made his stomach tighten thinking about showing up at the Harlem Club as a protest. He just wanted to hear Lenny, not make a scene. Or get in trouble with his parents.

When they pulled into the club's parking lot after dropping off Sylvia, Melvin's stomach felt like it had been turned inside out. What had he done, convincing his brother to bring them there? White people thronged toward the entrance. There was a whole line of them waiting to get in. The giant sign on the roof still flashed above them, but the first *e* had gone out so that it read, "Din-DANCE" instead of "Dine-DANCE." Clearly, Mr. Jones hadn't replaced it yet.

"You sure about this, Melvin?" Chuck said. They sat there looking at the crowded entrance.

He wasn't sure at all, but he didn't want to back out now.

"It'll be fine," Melvin said, surprising himself with how confident he sounded. He got out of the car. "Buh-be right back."

He didn't exactly have a plan, but he knew he needed to start in the kitchen. As usual, it felt like walking into a warm oven and smelled like Thanksgiving and Christmas rolled into one. Big-band music wafted through the air along with the savory aromas of roasted chicken and ham. Waiters left the kitchen with trays balanced on one gloved hand, the other gloved hand behind their backs, like the ushers at church. Mom would probably say it was the *only* similarity between the Harlem Club and Bethel A.M.E., but Melvin didn't think so. The Thirteen Black Cats' music was pretty transporting. He couldn't wait to see Lenny's face when they showed up in the dining room!

Sulli noticed him first. "Well, look who's here. Mr. Slick!" The others looked up from their work, and out came a chorus of compliments over how fine he looked in his suit, tie, and boutonniere.

Mrs. Carini came over, wiping her hands on the cloth tied around her waist. She hugged him. "Hello, Melvin. It's good to see you, but why are you here? Aren't you supposed to be at the Homecoming?"

"Wwwwe were. I wuh-wanted to hear Lenny. Do you think we cuh-cuh-cuh—" He jerked his head. "Could we come in?"

"Who is we?" Her forehead creased, whether in concern or simple inquiry, Melvin couldn't tell.

"Mmmmy buh-brother and ssssister . . . and a couple friends."

The creases remained. If she hadn't been concerned before, she was now. And maybe a little sad. He could tell from her eyes. "And your friends . . . also Negro?"

He nodded.

She inhaled deeply. Her eyes glinted. She looked suddenly determined. "I will talk to Mr. Jones. We will make a way. But bring them through the kitchen."

Melvin grinned. "Thhhhanks, Mrs. Carini."

He made a beeline for the car, choosing not to see anyone around him or notice whether they saw him. At the car, he told everyone to follow him. Marian looked worried, but Eugenia got out without hesitation.

A few people at the entrance looked their way, but a spark from the top of the sign turned everyone's attention to the roof and off them. Melvin led the group around the side and into the building.

The kitchen suddenly seemed smaller with all five of them standing in it. Mrs. Freeman straightened from where she'd been bending over an open oven and gasped. "Children, what in God's name do you think you're doing?" She knew them all from church, except for Catholic Bubba, but she knew his family. "Do your parents know you're here?"

"Yes, ma'am."

Melvin stared at his brother in disbelief. Chuck was lying to Mrs. Freeman, a mother of the church?

"We came to hear Lenny play," Chuck said.

"Not your uncle?" A hint of reproach gilded Mrs. Freeman's tone.

"Uncle Toussaint is here?" Marian asked. She exchanged a worried look with Chuck. Of course their uncle hadn't told them he was in town. After the last heated exchange between him and Pops, why would he have?

"Subbing for one of the trumpet players, I heard." Mrs. Freeman turned to stir her pan of gravy.

Mr. Jones entered the kitchen from the hallway that led to the dining room. Mrs. Carini followed. Melvin tried to read his expression. He wore a toothy grin, but what would come out of his mouth? An invitation to join the diners, or a cheerful apology and a boot from the premises?

"A pleasure to see you again, Melvin. A pleasure, all of you." He glanced around the group. "As you know, we have a policy."

Melvin felt Eugenia bristle beside him. Bubba nudged him from behind. Did he want Melvin to speak or to admit defeat and go?

"However," he said, glancing at Mrs. Carini, who looked at him expectantly, "we will be glad to accommodate you this time—seeing that it is a special night." He looked at Marian. "Congratulations, Miss Robinson, on the honor."

"Thank you." She beamed. It was working! They were going to be seated in the dining room. On a Saturday night. After Pops skinned their hides for going behind his back, he would be proud of them.

"Follow me, please. Ladies first." Mr. Jones led them down the hall and through the double doors. The place was *packed*. If Melvin had to guess, he'd say there were at least three hundred people there! Most were sitting at tables, talking and laughing and eating by candlelight, but at least sixty or seventy were on the dance floor, dancing to the blaring swing music. Uncle T stood with the trumpet section, blowing his horn with the rest of the Black Cats under the bright stage lights. His gold rings flashed as he worked the valves.

A brown face amidst all the white stopped Melvin's scanning of the crowd. He looked more closely. Was that—? It was. Will Thompson. *The Cobbler?* What was he doing here on a Saturday night? Maybe his local celebrity status made him an automatic exception to the rule. Melvin hoped the baseball player wouldn't see him, and if he did,

Melvin *doubly* hoped he wouldn't remember him from their embarrassing first *and* last encounter.

Five chairs had been lined up along the back wall. Melvin worried Chuck (or maybe Eugenia) might say something about not being given a table, but they each took a seat. Melvin stayed standing, trying to see through the dancing crowd, but it was no use. He stood on his chair. There was his friend—right in the front row. *Wailing!* Lenny leaned so far forward he looked like he might tumble from his seat. His foot tapped in time to the music.

Eugenia climbed onto the chair next to Melvin, bopping to the band's "sizzling syncopation." She said something but the music was too loud for him to hear.

He leaned her way.

"They're really good!" she said into his ear.

He nodded, grinning. Yes, they were.

The song ended and Miss Inez handed the microphone to Gene, laughing as people in the crowd whistled, clapped, and shouted for more.

"All right, all right, all my cool cats . . . this is your chance to get back to your tables and finish up your food, because it's time to welcome to the dance floor, your favorites and mine . . . Let's give it up for the soft-shoe styling of Little Butch and Delilah Jones!"

That's when Lenny saw Melvin, standing on his chair. Lenny's grin grew, and suddenly he was waving in their direction. A current of turning heads rippled through the restaurant.

Melvin scrambled down, his ears pounding from the reverberations of the music—but also from fear that they'd been seen. He helped Eugenia to the floor and they sat.

If anyone had noticed them, Melvin hoped to high heaven those people would go right back to their reveling and forget they were there. The crowd applauded and whistled as a boy in a suit and bow tie and a girl in a yellow ruffled dress appeared from offstage, their faces as shiny as the wax floor under their feet. Gene counted off the band and the music was bebopping again. The kids shuffled and slid in time to the music.

When the audience began throwing dollar bills onto the floor, Melvin and Bubba looked at each other across Eugenia, their eyes wide. By the looks of it, those two little kids made more money in an evening than Melvin had made in his lifetime! He climbed back onto his chair and got so into the performance and the cheering of the crowd that he stopped worrying about whether he was supposed to be there.

Until he heard yelling above the sound of the music.

Mr. Jones stood before a white man who was only inches from his face, shouting . . . and pointing to where Melvin and the others stood. He jabbed his finger in the Cobbler's direction next, and then into Mr. Jones's chest.

Melvin didn't have to hear the man's words to know what he was saying. Bubba tapped Melvin on the arm and looked toward the door, but Melvin felt like the deer he'd once seen Pops shoot: frozen in the face of his imminent death.

The music died out slowly, like Melvin's accordion when he stopped pumping but kept his finger on a chord button.

"You know who keeps this place open, right? We don't want them dancing on the same floor!"

Huh, Melvin thought. A moment before they'd been throwing money at two Negro kids doing that very thing.

Uncle T had made his way down from the bandstand and was headed toward the conflict. Chuck started to join him, but Marian pulled him back, pleading with her eyes.

"Next thing you know there'll be whites and coloreds dancing *together*!"

Uncle T was in the white man's face. "And what would be wrong with that, you ignorant son of a—?"

People started to head for the front doors, abandoning whole plates of food, Melvin couldn't help but notice.

"What'd you call me?" The man shoved Uncle T, who was as movable as a brick wall. Big mistake.

Uncle T popped him in the face. Blood spurted from the man's nose as he toppled backward, overturning a table. There were screams as more tables fell from the rush of people trying to get away.

"We should get out of here, Melvin," Eugenia said. Melvin looked to the stage, where Lenny had his arms around the two youngest Joneses, as if trying to shelter them from the fighting and from the man's hateful words.

Melvin sniffed the air. It smelled like smoke. His eyes darted around the room, trying to find the source. Had an overturned candle lit something on fire?

A man shouted from near the front door, "Fire! Fire on the roof! Get out!"

People were pushing, falling, scrabbling toward the door. Screams filled the building. Melvin tried to find Lenny, but the crowd was too thick. Across the room, the ceiling was dropping bits of burning plaster. More screams. More smoke. Someone was pulling on Melvin's arm. Bubba.

"Melvin! Come on, let's move!" Bubba shouted.

Mrs. Carini held open the door. The five of them rushed through, Melvin last. She grabbed his arm. "Lenny! Have you seen my *Lenny*?"

He shook his head helplessly. She gave one last look into the dining room and then scooted them down the long white hallway, like a hen with her chicks.

CHAPTER TWENTY-SEVEN

veryone needs to get out—*now!*" Mrs. Carini commanded the kitchen crew.

For a moment, they all looked like wax dummies in a museum.

"I said, go! There's a fire!"

The news registered and everyone moved at once, skittering toward the exit. Melvin looked over his shoulder. Mrs. Carini was running back toward the dining room, undoubtedly seeking Lenny. Should he help her?

"Come *on*, Melvin! We need to go!" Marian grabbed his hand and pulled him along. When they reached the vestibule, however, Melvin peeled away, taking the stairs two at a time.

Chuck shouted, "Melvin! *Melvin!* What are you doing?"

"Melvin! Get back here!" Marian screamed.

Footsteps echoed after him but he didn't stop until he was through the door of Lenny's apartment, standing in front of the glass chest. His heart pounded and his fingers shook as he opened the door and grabbed the silver goblet. He was reaching for the framed photo of Lenny's dad when Chuck grabbed him by the arm.

"We need to get out of here, Melvin!"

Sirens wailed in the distance. Smoke had started to pour into the apartment. Melvin glanced out the window. He couldn't see flames, but the air glowed with a spooky orange light. "Here." Melvin shoved the goblet and photo into Chuck's chest and ran to Lenny's bedroom, coughing from the thick, acrid smell. He grabbed his accordion case and headed for the door. "Okay!"

He and Chuck flew down the stairs to where Marian was still standing, tears streaming down her face. She hit Melvin in the arm. "Why did you do that? No instrument is worth risking your life!" she shrieked.

"Come on, let's go," Chuck said, and they fled through the back door into the cool night air.

The parking lot was crowded with people. White patrons and Negro servers had intermingled. They stared at the bright flames as if there were a giant bonfire atop the building. Chuck led Melvin and Marian to the car, where Bubba and Eugenia stood watching.

"That was crazy, man," Bubba said, sounding out of breath. He continued babbling, but Melvin was only partially listening. *Where was Lenny?*

Flames engulfed the "Dine-DANCE" sign. In only a matter of minutes, the famous lights would be swallowed up forever. Two red fire engines rolled in and men jumped off, pulling lengths of hose with them. They shouted at the crowd to get in their cars and leave, that it wasn't safe to be there.

People still stumbled out of the building, coughing and hacking, terror etched on their faces. What if the roof caved in? How many were still inside?

Mr. Jones helped women and men down the front steps, as did the Cobbler and a few of the Black Cats: Buick, Idaho, Gene. Melvin scanned the crowd. No sign of Uncle T. Melvin hoped he had made a run for it. His uncle had enough problems. He didn't also need to wind up in jail. *And where was Lenny?*

Melvin's eyes landed on the heads of the rest of the band. He dropped his case and strode toward them.

"Melvin!" Marian called, but he kept on. He nudged his way through the crowd until he reached the musicians. All of them held their instruments, as if they were extensions of their arms; they wouldn't leave them in a burning building any more than they would leave their grannies. Except for Mitch, the drummer, poor guy.

Melvin pushed past Mitch into the center of the group, and there he was, Lenny, his mom on one side and Miss Inez on the other. Lenny's arm draped around his mom's shoulders; her arm wrapped around his waist.

"Lenny!" He grabbed his friend and hugged him, then let go just as quickly, afraid the guys in the band might think he was a big sap. But they were slapping him on the back, saying they were glad he was all right and what was he doing there, anyway?

"Jjjjjust came to see y'all play," he said, glancing around the circle.

Mrs. Carini spoke softly. "You must get home. Your family will be worried if they hear the news."

Well, no they won't, he thought, since they don't actually know we're here.

Still, she was right. They should be heading home . . . something Lenny and his mom could no longer do. "You hhhhhave nuh-nowhere to sssssstay."

"We will be fine," Mrs. Carini said. "But you should go. The fireman said it's not safe."

Chuck appeared in the circle then. "Melvin?"

Mrs. Carini saw the goblet and frame in Chuck's hands. "What is this?" She looked at Chuck and then Melvin. "You saved these from our apartment?" She looked at him in awe.

He took the objects from Chuck and handed them to her, nodding. "Yyyou can come to *our* house. Mmmy puh-puh-parents would want you to . . ."

Mrs. Carini wrapped her free arm around him. Her black curls tickled his face. Melvin felt himself growing warm. "Thank you, Melvin. You are very kind."

* * *

They were silent on the way to Eugenia's place. Clearly, no one knew what to say. Right before she got out of the car, Chuck spoke. "You don't have to keep this a secret for us. We'll be telling our parents where we were."

We will? Melvin broke out in a cold sweat. Of course they had to tell Mom and Pops, but still, he wasn't looking forward to it.

Eugenia nodded and got out. "Thank you for escorting me, Melvin. It was . . . memorable." She turned serious. "And tell your friends I'm sorry about their apartment."

Melvin nodded in return. It was quiet the rest of the way home.

As soon as they pulled into the driveway, Mom came running outside. He stayed put in the back seat, while Mom embraced Marian. "Of course, you will always be a queen to us," she was saying as Melvin got out of the car, keeping his eyes on the ground. Suddenly, his arms were pinned to his sides. Now Mom was hugging him. "Thank God you are okay," she exhaled into his ear.

Maisy rushed out and threw her arms around them both with a sob. They were acting as if they already knew. *Did they?*

"Your uncle," Mom said, seeming to read his mind. "He called and told us about the fire. Said he saw you at the club." She held him at arm's length. "You got a whole lot of explainin' to do, young man!" she snapped, then went right back to squeezing him so that he could hardly breathe, let alone explain anything.

Pops appeared on the front porch, his face as wooden as a carved statue. What was their dad thinking? Didn't really matter. Bottom line: they were in trouble.

Mom finally released Melvin from her vise grip.

"May I take Bubba home, Mama?"

Mama? Chuck hadn't called her *Mama* since they were little.

"You may. Francis, I trust you will tell your parents where you were tonight." The message was clear: if he didn't, she would.

"Yes, ma'am," Bubba said in a low voice. "See you later, Melvin."

Melvin lifted his hand to say goodbye. He didn't have it in him to try and get any words out.

A car door shutting caused everyone to turn.

Lenny and Mrs. Carini stood on the sidewalk. Her white-gloved hands clutched her purse handles. The awkward silence stretched into what felt like minutes.

Mom broke the spell that seemed to have come over them all. "Hello, Lenny. This is a surprise. Is this your mother?"

Melvin realized with a start that his parents had never actually met Lenny's mom. "Mmmmom, Puh-Pops, this is Mrs. Carini."

Mom rushed to welcome them. "Well, it's wonderful to meet you, finally. I'm Claudine." She shook Mrs. Carini's hand. "Claudine Robinson. And these are my other children: Charles, Marian, and Margaret." Maisy made a face at the sound of her real name. "Their friend, Francis, and my husband, Claude Robinson."

Pops bowed his head. "Pleasure, Mrs. Carini."

"Please . . . call me Reby," Mrs. Carini said.

The awkwardness returned as they all stood looking at one another.

"Forgive my manners," Mom said. "It's too cold to be doing introductions on the front lawn. Would you care to come in?"

Mrs. Carini glanced between Melvin and his mom. "I'm sorry. You did not realize we were coming. We should go." She started to turn.

"Wait!" Melvin shouted.

"I should get Bubba home," Chuck said. No doubt he was in a hurry to get out of there before the bomb of where Lenny lived dropped. He and Bubba got in the car.

While Chuck was backing out of the driveway, Melvin worked up the courage to tell his parents what he should have told them long before then. "Lenny and his mmmmom . . . they live at the Hhhharlem Club." He looked at Lenny, who stood with his hands clasped in front of him, not saying a word. "They have nuh-nowhere to go."

Mom's hands covered her mouth, but not before a small "oh" sound escaped.

Maisy's eyes were as big as Pops's cocktail coasters. "You *live* at the Harlem Club? Does that mean you know the Thirteen Black

Cats—personally?" No doubt Maisy was already thinking about an interview with the band.

Melvin looked at her sternly and knocked her shoulder. This was *not* the time.

"I'm so sorry," Mom said. "You must come in. Please."

"Ma," Lenny muttered, motioning toward the door with his head. He took her by the elbow and they walked the concrete path. The rest of them tramped up the steps behind them and into the house. Pops held the screen door.

"We'll be talkin' later," Pops said. His breath smelled faintly of pipe smoke. Melvin ducked his head and entered, glad to be home—to *have* a home—but not at all looking forward to what was coming.

CHAPTER TWENTY-EIGHT

nside, Pops offered Lenny and his mom a seat on the couch. Marian excused herself to change her clothes and Maisy trailed along, asking a million questions about the dance. No doubt she would interrogate Marian about the Harlem Club as soon as they were behind closed doors.

"Would you like some water, or milk?" Mom asked. "Perhaps a cup of tea . . . Reby?"

Mrs. Carini placed her gloves over the top of her purse on the floor. "Water is fine, thank you."

"I'd take some milk," Lenny said. His mom looked at him sharply. "Please."

Mom left for the kitchen, and to Melvin's surprise, Pops followed her. He didn't usually participate in serving guests; that was Mom's job.

"You have a very nice home, Melvin," Mrs. Carini said, her eyes roaming the living room.

"Thank you." He sat on the floor, legs crossed, hands fidgeting. "You ssssounded rrrreally good tonight."

Lenny smiled briefly. "I did, didn't I?"

It was quiet again, except for the sound of water running in the sink and the clinking of milk bottles. Melvin heard his parents retreat farther into the dining area. They spoke in tones too low to make out the words.

Lenny broke the silence. "Ma, do you think . . ." His voice sounded choked. "All our things . . . Did we lose them all?" Melvin watched his friend with concern.

Mrs. Carini smiled tenderly at her son and put her hand on his leg. "As you have said, they are only *things*, caro, my dear one. If we did, they can be replaced. Baruch Hashem, thanks to God, we are alive."

Lenny's forehead wrinkled in contemplation. Melvin wished he could read his friend's thoughts. Then Lenny said quietly, "Ah-main." It sounded much different from how worshippers at Bethel A.M.E. said it—*Ay-MEN!*—shouting it like exclamation points at the end of the preacher's truest and most inspired statements, but Melvin recognized it regardless. It was the same word, with the same desire attached.

Amen. May it be so.

The others returned to the living room: Mom, Pops, Marian, and Maisy, who carried a blanket. Mom set the drinks on coasters on the coffee table, and then eyed Maisy. "Would you like a blanket?" Maisy asked shyly.

Mrs. Carini reached for it. "Thank you, bubbeleh."

Maisy cocked her head at her.

Melvin knew she wanted to ask about the unfamiliar word but was trying to be respectful. "It means 'sweetheart,'" he said. "In Yiddish." He exchanged a smile with Mrs. Carini.

Maisy snuggled up to Melvin on the floor and wrapped her arms around him again. "I was so scared, brother. I don't ever want to lose you."

"I don't wwwwwant to lose me either." The others laughed in response.

Pops spoke from his chair; Mom stood by his shoulder. "Claudine and I would like you and your son to stay here, at least until you can find something more permanent. We know our boys have become good friends."

Mrs. Carini started to protest, but Lenny cut her off. "Ma, they are offering their *home*. Don't you always tell me . . . Hashem will provide?"

She looked intently at Pops. "That is very kind. We will accept—for one night only. We do not want to intrude."

"All right. Tomorrow you can assess the situation, but please, you are welcome to stay for as long as you need."

Mrs. Carini looked intently at him again. "Mr. Robinson," she began.

"Claude," he said.

"All right. Claude." She cleared her throat. "Seeing how fate has brought us together through these challenging circumstances, I feel I must introduce myself again. More properly."

The energy in the room felt suddenly taut, like Melvin's vocal cords before he tried to speak.

"I am Rebecca Friedman. And this is my son, Leonardo, son of Ariel." She gazed at him meaningfully.

A look of sudden recognition flickered across Pops's face. His thin fingers tightened on his armrests, almost imperceptibly. It was as if the room itself were holding its breath. Melvin, too, felt breathless as he pieced together the significance of what Mrs. Carini had revealed. The photo. Ariel. *Friedman*. Lenny.

"I . . ." Pops began. "I don't know what to say." He looked at Lenny. "Except that I see him now. My . . ." His voice had caught on something. "My friend."

Mom made a sound, half sob, half laugh. "Well, then, our home truly is also your home, isn't it?"

Marian and Maisy looked at each other, confused.

"*Ariel*," Melvin said to Maisy. He sprang to his feet, ran to his room, and returned with the photo of Pops and the boy with the silver goblet. He handed it to Mrs. Carini.

"Ariel," she whispered, grazing the photo with her fingertips.

"Ma?" Lenny looked at her.

Her eyes glistened. "This is a picture of your father. I presume on the day of his bar mitzvah. What a lovely picture."

"And . . ." Lenny looked at Pops. "Is this *you*?"

"It is."

"So, the kiddush cup in this picture," Lenny said, "is the same one that Melvin saved from our apartment."

"It is." Mrs. Carini smiled at Melvin.

Melvin took a deep breath. "Beshert," he said, looking at Lenny. "Our friendship was . . . meant to be."

The back door opened and shut. Chuck appeared. "Come on in, son," Pops said. "I want you *all* to hear this." Chuck parked himself in a chair on the other side of Mom. "These good people are the family of one of my childhood friends." Chuck's eyes registered his surprise. "I haven't seen Ariel in many years, of course. But I think about him every day." Pops looked at Mrs. Carini. "I was sorry to hear of his passing. He made the ultimate sacrifice."

"He knew it was likely," Mrs. Carini said. "He went to fight Hitler anyway. He was a man of conviction."

"Undeniably. I planned to be there alongside him, but got turned away. Didn't pass the medical."

Had Pops been sick in some way? Why hadn't he passed the military's medical exam? Melvin had always thought of his dad as sinewy and tough, able to track deer for miles and hit golf balls two hundred yards or more. Looking at him reclined in his chair, suddenly his limbs were thin, possibly breakable.

"See, family, Ariel Friedman and I were good friends in high school. We both wanted to go to college, but then the banks went belly up and I lost all my savings." Melvin and Maisy eyed each other but kept their mouths shut. They had never said anything to Pops about the diary.

"Ariel offered me some money to attend, but I turned him down. He went on and finished school, got a good job working for a bank. When he heard I was trying to buy a home for my young family and that I was having difficulty because of *where* I wanted to buy it, he pretended *he* was the buyer, got the house, and then deeded it over to me so it could be legally mine."

Marian gasped. "*This* house?"

"This very one."

"I don't understand, Daddy. Why were you having difficulty buying a house here?" Maisy asked.

"He's saying because we're a Negro family, they didn't want us in this neighborhood," Chuck said, his resentment barely concealed beneath his older-wiser-brother tone of voice.

"That's right," Pops said.

"That's *not* right!" Maisy exclaimed. "It's cruel! And pigheaded. And unfair. People can't tell you where you can live and where you can't. Can they?"

Melvin appreciated that Pops didn't interrupt Maisy but let her rant until she was through.

"Well, they sure think they can. And it has been effective for a long time at keeping people separate."

"But Grandma lived in this neighborhood before we did," Marian pointed out. "How is that?"

"Oh, that man she married, after your grandfather left," Mom said. "You probably barely remember him, but he was a very light-skinned man. The realtor never asked and he didn't tell. The man no doubt thought he was selling to a white man."

"And to be honest," Mrs. Carini interjected, "Jewish people have been the objects of this same kind of discrimination. But because my Ariel had a job at the bank, the realtor knew him and 'overlooked' his Jewish background. I realized who you were when Lenny told me your address this evening, since I have been seeing this return address on your envelopes every month for the past fourteen years."

"What does she mean, Daddy?" Maisy asked. "You've been sending Lenny's mom mail?"

"Loan repayments. Monthly, to a post office box in the name of Rebecca Friedman."

"Yes, and now, I am happy to say, your father has paid it all back. As of this month, this house is one hundred percent the Robinsons'!"

"And it will also always be yours," Pops said.

Melvin's head was spinning, stunned by this most recent revelation. He'd always seen his neighborhood as a safe place, his home. Now he wondered, Was it really these things?

"Is it still hard for Negro people to get homes wherever they want?" Maisy asked. She looked around the room. The adults exchanged glances.

Pops exhaled. "Well, now, Maisy, it's—"

"Someone needs to do something about this!" Maisy exclaimed. "It's unjust!"

Chuck spoke again. "That's the point, Maisy. Someone *did* do something. Lenny's dad did. Our dad did. And now we live here."

Maisy looked like she might cry.

"'So every bondman in his own hand bears the power to cancel his captivity.' Casca, *Julius Caesar*." Pops's roaming eyes stopped on Melvin, his gaze so intense it could have pierced armor. "None of us need be prisoner to our circumstances."

Pops had done it, Melvin thought, together with Lenny's dad: He had played a part in canceling his own captivity, refused to be a prisoner to circumstance. He had taken a stand and broken down a part of the wall. Melvin had not realized how high that wall stood. Or how brave his pops was. Until now.

Pops turned to Mrs. Carini again. "If it's not too personal to ask, did you remarry? Your last name . . ."

"It's not too personal, and no, I never remarried. I use my maiden name because I don't want my son to be harassed for being Jewish."

Pops nodded with understanding.

It was as if Melvin's eyes had been opened and he couldn't close them again, like when the scales fell from Saul's sightless eyes in the Bible. Once blind to discrimination, suddenly Melvin was seeing it everywhere—as close as his own neighborhood.

But he saw something else too. People coming together to help other people, as fellow humans. Mom got on the phone and called neighbors—the Bertos, the Balduccis, the Butlers, the Lambs—and other friends—the Purcells, the Dalberts, the Carters, the Jessups. Those they knew from Bethel A.M.E., the NAACP, the Prince Hall Freemasons, and Wednesday Art Club. Their circle—Negro and white—looked out for each other in times of need. They would look out for the Carini-Friedmans, as well. They were each other's mishpachah, no matter which side of town they lived on.

CHAPTER TWENTY-NINE

Melvin was on the shiny dance floor at the Harlem Club. Grass huts and palm trees surrounded the stage. The white faces in the audience smiled and cheered. Some even threw dollar bills. He whirled and slid and moved his feet to the big-band music, coming from a pride of instrument-playing lions. The exhilaration was phenomenal. But the music started moving too fast. He couldn't keep up. He stumbled over his own feet. He tripped and fell to his knees. When he looked up, the crowd was no longer cheering. Their faces were twisted in hatred. They shouted and raised their fists. "It's that Till boy!" someone shouted. They advanced, circling round. They were upon him, pummeling him, kicking and jumping on him. Someone grabbed him by the shoulder. Someone was shaking him.

"Hey! Melvin!"

He opened his eyes with a start. Chuck squatted at the side of his bunk. "You were shaking the bed with all your thrashing around." He moved toward the door. "It's time to get up anyway. Church."

Melvin lay there, recovering from the bad dream. It took him a moment to realize he was shivering. Mr. Jones and his Harlem Club hadn't brought segregation to Spokane. It had been there already. In the hearts of people who didn't want his family to live in the same neighborhood with them . . . who didn't want races to mix.

And it wasn't only in the past (which wasn't that far past).

It was in the Spokane Club, where his grandma had to enter through the back and Pops could never belong.

It was in a woman who refused to visit a dentist who also treated Negroes.

It was in the clerk who hid in the back of the store while a Negro woman waited for service.

And in the man who took up more space in his seat when Melvin got on the bus.

Maybe it wasn't in everyone, but it was here, and it was enough to bring out the worst in people.

He put his feet on the floor, rubbed his eyes. Normally, he didn't mind church—he got to sing, after all—but today he didn't feel like it. How many people would know about them being at the Harlem Club, thanks to Mrs. Freeman? They would no doubt get an earful from other churchgoers. And when was Pops going to dole out their punishment?

Ultimately, the smell of frying eggs and bacon got him moving. He came into the kitchen a while later, dressed in his button-up shirt, blue V-neck sweater, and pants that Mom had ironed with so much starch he feared the sound of them cracking would be heard church-wide every time he sat and stood during the service. Lenny and his mom were already seated at the table and greeted him with *good mornings*. Pops had taken Marian and Maisy to Grandma's late last night, where they would stay as long as the Carinis needed a bed.

"Well, hello there, sleepyhead," Mom said, handing out plates of food.

Pops and Chuck joined them, and they all held hands and bowed their heads. "Thank you for this food which we are about to receive. Use it for the nourishment of our bodies. And thank you for our guests. Amen." It was Pops's standard meal prayer with the added part about their guests.

"So, I was thinking more about what you told us last night, Pops," Chuck said. "And I was wondering, what happened after you moved in? I mean, if we weren't supposed to buy a house here, I'm guessing not everyone was happy when we showed up."

Melvin had had the same thought.

"You guessed right, son."

"Let me tell *you*," Mom began. She'd been relatively quiet the night before, but this morning she seemed eager to continue the story. "'Not happy' is an understatement! There were people who were *so* unhappy, they circulated a petition to get us removed. And when your father brought us to see our new home for the first time—Melvin you weren't born yet, but you were on your way—every single window had been smashed in. Every one. Quite a welcome."

Mrs. Carini was shaking her head. "Oh, that is *awful*. Simply awful."

"Your father sent us to Grandma Robinson's while he cleaned up the glass and then slept on the floor of the living room with his shotgun in case the jackal who did it decided to make another call."

"Did you fffffffind out who it was?" Melvin asked.

"Never did," Mom said. "But that's all right because the good *Lord* knows. That person will have to make an account for his actions."

Mom had put down her fork long ago. She had more to say. "We moved in all our belongings. Then I got down on my knees"—her voice rose with conviction—"and prayed to God that He would fight against those who were fighting us."

Soon after that, she said, a particularly surly neighbor came home from work, sat in his armchair, and keeled over from a heart attack! Another family's son got struck with polio. Another family's dog died.

Melvin couldn't believe what was coming from his mom's mouth. "Do you really thhh . . . think God would give a child puh-puh-polio because his parents were mmmmean?"

"What I know is that I prayed, and one by one, those mean people disappeared."

Mrs. Carini chimed in. "The Torah tells us that, yes, Hashem is long-suffering and his love and mercy endure forever, but also that the sins of the fathers will be visited on their children. God sends us many blessings, but because of human choices, there are also curses. There are consequences to our actions."

The law of cause and effect—that's what Mr. Farber would call it. They had talked about it in science class.

What had caused the effect of his tongue having so much trouble forming the many words that leapt through his mind, leaving him breathless and feeling feeble? What had caused his mouth to break? Was he bearing the consequence of some forefather's sin? Was *he* cursed?

He didn't know, but he believed Mr. Farber. Whatever caused him to trip and stumble, to get stuck on his words, *it wasn't his fault.* And regardless of what anyone before him had done, he could choose his own, new actions. Actions that would reverberate for good. If there *were* a curse, it would be avoiding things he wanted to do just because he was afraid of looking or sounding stupid.

He cleared his dishes and looked at the clock on the wall. There was still time. "I'll buh-be back in time for church!" he said, and rushed out before anyone could stop him. He went to his room before leaving the house.

Tuck sat on his little island, surrounded by water, and four plastic walls. Melvin lifted him to eye level, committing every detail of his turtle to memory. He stroked Tuck's hard yellow-brown shell, which had always reminded him of Pops's bottom teeth, stained from his pipe smoking. Tuck had two, bright red, oblong markings on either side of his face. Very dapper. Along his head and neck, stripes of different hues of green outlined in black reminded Melvin of map elevation markings. He stared into Tuck's still eye, with its pupil that looked like a silhouette of Saturn surrounded by a glassy, green marble. A whole universe was there in his turtle's eye. He deserved more than these four walls.

"Ready, little guy? Let's go do this." He cupped Tuck in his hands and headed for the front door.

Outside, the air was crisp; the sharpness of it cut away any last vestiges of sleep. Layers of brown, orange, and yellow leaves circled the few barren trees that stood along the sidewalk like colorful versions of Grandma's fancy doilies. Melvin's eyes roamed the street as he walked and thought about who lived in each house.

With only one exception—Old Man Pritchard, who was certifiably crazy, anyhow, and had a problem with the bottle—*everyone* on their street had been good, kind, and respectful. In his experience, at least, not one of them had ever shown the least ill will toward his family or complained about their presence on Empire Avenue, although his stomach still clenched at the thought of Mr. Hatchett's comment the day Chuck had knocked Gary down at the North Pole. *Not those kind of Negroes.*

Still, Melvin's experience on their street was a sign that things *could* change for the better.

A few morning birds trilled from the cherry tree in Millie's front yard. They sounded like hope. He walked up the Takazawas' front steps, holding Tuck in the protective shell of his hands, as if the reptile were back inside an egg waiting to hatch. He pulled the hand underneath Tuck into his chest and knocked on the door lightly, in case anyone was still asleep, although he knew the family usually rose early to open their market.

Millie came to the door. Her lips curved in a small smile. A friendly smile. "Hello, Melvin."

"Hello"—he took a breath and exhaled—"Millie." He liked the way her name came out a little bit airy, floating, the way she made him feel.

"I heard about Lenny," she said. "My family wanted him to have these." She indicated a box full of fresh vegetables near the door—different shades of green, orange, yellow, and brown. "Will you be seeing him soon?" That's when she noticed his hands were occupied. "Oh! You have a turtle!"

"Yes, a living one," he said, wondering if she would catch the reference to her stone turtle, which he had continued to carry in his pocket every day to school. "Would you . . . would you like to get a malt at the North Pole sometime?" His heart thrilled at how fluidly the question had come out.

"I would love to," she said, and he thought he might faint on the spot.

"Great." He turned to leave.

"When?" she said quickly.

"Oh, right. FFFFriday after school?"

"Sure. Can you take these vegetables now? Or do you need to take your turtle home and come back?"

Tuck! He had almost forgotten. "I was wondering if you . . . you could . . . would you put him in your pond? I wwwwant him to be free."

She smiled and held out her hands.

CHAPTER THIRTY

In November, the Carinis moved into the home Will Thompson had been renting. He'd been traded and would be playing for a different minor league team. Before the Cobbler left, Melvin had worked up the courage to ask him for throwing lessons for him and Lenny, who had confided to Melvin that not having a dad to teach him, he'd never felt very sure of himself with a ball.

In the midst of getting their lesson, the Carinis' situation had come up. The Cobbler had told them he was moving (a scoop that he'd shared with Maisy for her new newspaper, the *Inland Empire Inquirer*) and everything had fallen into place. The Carinis were officially neighbors—across the way from Grandma Robinson on Providence Street, just around the corner from Melvin's family.

Mrs. Carini had gotten a new job cooking at the Spokane Club through Grandma Robinson, and Pops's Prince Hall Grand Masonic Lodge had given the Carinis a loan to help them pay the first month's rent and replace their damaged furniture. So all was golden there.

One Saturday morning, Lenny showed up on their front porch unannounced. Melvin answered the door.

"Hi, Lenny . . . what's up?" Lenny was wearing the same kind of small, black cap that Melvin had first seen in the photo of Pops and Lenny's dad.

"I decided to attend shul this morning. Ma had to work, so I thought I'd see if you wanted to walk with me." Melvin had learned from Lenny and his mom that a shul—or synagogue—was like church for Jewish people.

Melvin turned to ask Pops if it was okay.

Pops appeared from behind his newspaper. "Sounds fine to me. As long as you're back shortly to do your Saturday morning job." Of course, Pops wouldn't let him forget: Big Bertha needed her bath.

"Okay!" He closed the door behind them. They headed down Empire. "So . . . the hat . . . why do you wear it?"

"It's called a kippah. I decided I'm going to start wearing mine more. It's to remind us that Hashem is always above us, always watching. And to show our pride in being Jewish."

Melvin gave him a thumbs-up.

"I'm going today . . . for my dad. It's the anniversary of when he died."

Melvin clapped Lenny on the back, feeling for his friend. If he'd had a kippah he would have worn one to honor Ariel Friedman, too, the man responsible for his family's home.

They headed in the direction of Cleveland High, which was only a couple blocks from the synagogue. It felt good to walk down the street with a buddy. A lot had changed since that first day of school, three months before.

They reached the block of the Tiger's Den, the hangout across from the high school. A small knot of guys stood out front. Melvin recognized the greased-back blond hair of Gary Ratliff right away. Lenny nudged him with his elbow. "We can turn here—we don't have to go past them."

One thing that hadn't changed over three months was Gary's constant need to find ways to put Melvin down. Melvin was tired of walking around scared, trying to avoid Gary at all costs. "No." He steeled himself and kept walking, prepared to ignore whatever rude comments came out of the Rat's big mouth.

Troy nodded in their direction and Gary turned, just as Melvin and Lenny reached them. "Well, what do you know? Carini's a kike!"

Melvin didn't have any idea what Gary was talking about, but he could tell by the way he sneered and spat the last word that it wasn't a compliment. Before he knew what was happening, Gary had snatched the saucer-hat off Lenny, whose glasses got knocked to the ground. Gary waved the kippah overhead.

"Give it back!" Lenny shouted, holding his head where the cap had been. He bent over and picked up his glasses.

Gary had chosen Lenny—not him—to pick on. Stunned, Melvin stood there, not knowing what to do.

More kids came out of the Tiger's Den to watch someone who wasn't them be ridiculed. The little hat bobbed in Gary's hand as he waved it this way and that, avoiding Lenny's grabs for it.

Stop it! Melvin wanted to shout. Cut it out! Neither of the commands went farther than his brain cells. They stood at the base of his skull, stamping and shouting, demanding to be spoken. But his jaw muscles and lips were stuck shut.

Gary shoved Lenny, as if to get him to react. Lenny lost his balance and tumbled to the ground. A bomb detonated in Melvin's chest. He growled, and then he yelled, "Aaaahhhh!" as he plunged headfirst into Gary's middle. They flew for what felt like forever before hitting the ground with a bone-splitting crunch. Melvin raised his fist and Gary covered his face.

Someone grabbed Melvin's arm.

He looked up to see Lenny, shaking his head.

Melvin's chest heaved. He took the kippah from Gary's hand, put his knee in Gary's middle, and stood. Gary scrambled to his feet and started toward him.

Suddenly, something bigger and stronger than any of them was coursing through Melvin's veins. Like the mighty Spokane River. The spirit of Emmett Till, he thought. And then a voice in his ear: You are every bit as good as this boy.

He felt as if he had grown three inches. His heart beat steady and strong. His legs were rooted to the ground. He raised his chest to meet whatever came next. A line from a church song came into his mind, "Like a tree planted by the water, I shall not be moved." He gazed into Gary's eyes and realized: he wasn't afraid. There wasn't room for fear, because it'd been crowded out by love—for Lenny, for his own family, for his people and all they'd been through. Even for himself. Before him stood a lost and confused kid who'd swallowed a pack of lies and it was poisoning him.

Melvin reached out his hand. Would the boy see the antidote that it offered?

Gary's eyes narrowed. He yanked at the hem of his jacket to straighten it, and he walked away.

Melvin gave Lenny his kippah back. "Thanks for standing up for me," Lenny said.

"I wassss stuh-standing up for all of us." He remembered Pops's line: *So every bondman in his own hand bears the power to cancel his captivity*. From now on, that's what Melvin would be doing. And while he was pretty sure Gary wouldn't be giving them any trouble going forward, if he did, Melvin knew he could handle it.

* * *

On December 7, Melvin turned fourteen. He'd been born in 1941 on the "date which will live in infamy," according to President Franklin Delano Roosevelt. The day his uncle's and Lenny's dad's fates had been sealed. And Millie's family's forced removal was set into motion. And the clock started ticking on a hundred thousand Japanese who would perish beneath a mushroom cloud unlike anything the world had ever seen. The day America was pulled into a war that needed to be waged to defend Jewish people, like his friend Lenny, and *still*, millions of Jews had lost their lives in extermination camps.

His birthday was always a little somber, as his family at some point would make time to visit Uncle Melvin at the cemetery, and Grandma Robinson would dab her eyes with her handkerchief, and Pops would stand off to the side, silently. Melvin had always thought Pops's aloofness revealed a lack of caring, but it struck him this time around that more likely Pops was sad, and this was simply how he showed it.

The rest of December was a blur of wintry weather and coldness so fierce the snot froze up in Melvin's nose before it had a chance to run. On one of his dates with Millie at the North Pole soda fountain, Melvin joked that he felt like Matthew Henson—the first Negro man to reach the *real* North Pole, who had died earlier that year. Melvin had been reading about Henson and had decided he would visit every continent, even the poles, eventually.

Speaking was still hard, but being with Millie was always easy.

On that same outing, she told him her actual name. The Japanese name her grandparents still called her, even though her parents did not.

Michiko.

"Michiko," he said effortlessly. It rolled off his tongue. "What does it mmmmean?"

Her cheeks flushed pink. Her dimples showed. "Beautiful wisdom child."

"That's you, all right," he said, not even a bit embarrassed. "I think you should use that nuh-name *all* the time."

Her eyes radiated joy. "I think so too."

He worried aloud about Tuck freezing to death—his turtle wasn't used to life in the wild, after all—but she assured him that Tuck was doing just fine. He'd slipped under the water before it had frozen over and was hibernating at the bottom of the pond as turtles do in winter. Melvin always learned something new when he was with Millie-now-Michiko. *Beautiful wisdom child.*

* * *

The day before New Year's Eve—the January New Year, that is, as the Jewish one had begun back in September—Mrs. Carini insisted they all come to her and Lenny's new place, as a housewarming. "A new house isn't a home until it has welcomed guests," she told them.

That night, they all sat around the table and Mrs. Carini lit candles and then said a special prayer in Hebrew. When she was done, she translated for them: "It means 'Thanks be to God for sustaining us in life and bringing us safely to this moment.'" The Robinson family nodded in agreement.

Then Lenny, wearing his kippah, sang a prayer in Hebrew over his dad's silver kiddush cup, which had been filled with grape juice. He took a sip and passed the goblet to Melvin, who held the family heirloom with reverence. Each of them drank, and then Mrs. Carini blessed a big, fluffy-looking, golden-brown loaf of bread she called challah and sent pieces around the table.

Melvin couldn't help but notice it was a whole lot like what they did during Communion at Bethel A.M.E. Church: eating bread that had been broken (except Mrs. Carini's was a whole lot tastier!) and drinking from the same cup. Reverend Reed liked to say the ritual pointed to the truth that they were all in this life together. The ups and downs. The good and the bad. Melvin had a feeling he and Lenny would be riding the ups and downs as friends for a long time to come. Maybe forever.

A few weeks later, Pops came home from the NAACP meeting with news of an important gathering that would be convened at Calvary Baptist church. The committee had voted unanimously that Melvin and Lenny, their *Starlit Stairway* fame still lingering, were to play a duet—something appropriate for the setting, which meant *not* "It Don't Mean a Thing (If It Ain't Got That Swing)," of course.

Pops had more big news: he had volunteered Melvin to introduce the main speaker, a woman coming all the way from the South to talk about developments in the fight against segregation and unequal treatment of Negroes, and the fight *for* civil rights.

"Why me?" Melvin asked, his heart already palpitating at the thought of standing up in front of a large group of people to speak, even though he'd had a few speech lessons with Mrs. Farber and her exercises had been helping him a lot. More than Mr. Feuchtinger's, at least. He'd thrown the he-man booklet in the trash.

"Why *not* you?" Pops asked and walked out of the room, leaving Melvin alone with his thoughts.

That night, Melvin dreamed. He was used to dreams about things being stuck in his throat or mouth—a cherry bomb, a baseball. The most disgusting had been a tiger muskie, the giant, ugly fish with whiskers that he and Pops sometimes caught at Curlew Lake.

This one was also about his throat, but it was different. In this dream, Michiko came to him, reached her hand inside his mouth, and pulled out a large, gold skeleton key. As soon as the key was out, a ribbon of glittering gold began to stream from his mouth, the length of which piled up around him and then continued streaming, out of their house and down the street, as if it were conscious, animated, seeking out someone or something. Transmuted into a half-liquid, half-light kind of substance, it kept flowing from his mouth and wrapped around the people and houses it came upon, connecting everyone it touched. Like the strong and beautiful gold on a formerly broken kintsugi vase.

When he woke up, his whole face felt open, spacious. His tongue felt released. After that, he wasn't nervous about speaking at the church, even though he didn't know how it was going to go.

The evening of the event, Melvin and Lenny played their version of "I Shall Not Be Moved," which inspired everyone to sing along and received a standing ovation, including from members of the Thirteen Black Cats, who had arrived back in Spokane after touring the West Coast. Lenny had gotten to make a guest appearance at their latest show.

The applause died down, and Melvin stood alone at the pulpit. Calvary Baptist's sanctuary was bigger than Bethel A.M.E.'s and every pew was filled. His hands and legs and lips trembled.

He gripped the edges of the pulpit and looked out at the mostly brown faces of people who had known and cared for him his entire life: Mom and Pops. Marian, Maisy, and Chuck, who flashed him a grin. Grandma Robinson. The Jessups. The Strongs and Blackwells. The Carters. The Freemans, Purcells, and Dalberts. He recognized several of the Harlem Club's former staff, including Sulli.

Pops may have chosen to bust down a wall to buy a house, but their home was here too, with this community—some who had been born in Spokane, like his parents; others who had come from the South, seeking greater freedom.

Michiko sat a few rows back with her parents. Her bright eyes said, You can do this!

He knew he would get stuck on some of his words, and it was all right. He had decided the best way to deal with an enemy, if he could, was to make that enemy his friend. The Stutter was a part of what made him *him* and he was okay. Just the way he was.

Melvin took a deep breath, letting in the spirit of that something larger that flowed like the Spokane River, that something that connected them all. Then he opened his mouth to say what he *had* to say:

"Recently, I had to mmmmmake uh . . . a *choice*—to st—" Be still. Wait for the word. "To stand up to someone who's been puh-pushing me around . . . ssssssince I was uh . . . a *kid*." He wasn't a kid anymore; he knew that. "It wwwwasn't a hard choice, because this . . . this person, he had started pushing around my . . . my *friend*, too." He glanced at Lenny in the front pew with his mom. "I realized something when I . . . when I stood up to him . . . I realized . . . there is no *us* and *them*. There is only . . . only *us*. We are all in this tuh . . . together."

He looked out and saw two white faces in the crowd—Mr. and Mrs. Farber! His teacher gave him a thumbs-up.

"The woman I have the . . . the honor to introduce . . . knows this too. She asked a policeman, 'Why do you puh-puh-push us around?' and he had no good answer except to arrest her." Melvin had read all about it in *Jet* magazine. "I introduce to you, a wwwwwoman who would not be . . . be moved . . . Mrs. Rosa . . . Parks."

People applauded. Melvin waited until the diminutive woman had come all the way to the pulpit so he could shake her hand. This woman had stood her ground in the face of being bullied. She might have looked small, but she was mighty inside. She deserved honor and respect.

Just like me, Melvin thought.

Mrs. Parks looked him in the eye as they shook hands. "Well done, my son. Well done."

Ah-MAIN, Melvin thought. Amen.

AUTHOR'S NOTE

Dear Reader,

This story took root in my imagination when I was already grown up—at least thirty years old—and I heard my grandma recount how she and my grandpa acquired their home. They raised all four of their children in that house, including my dad, and I loved visiting them there on Empire Avenue in Spokane, Washington. I loved excavating the game closet in my dad and

My dad, age 9, and his siblings, 1954.

uncles' old room. I loved playing in the basement, where my grandpa kept his train set and model airplanes (and his at-home kidney dialysis machine—one of the first in the country—that my grandma put him on and monitored two to three times a week). I loved sitting in my grandpa's black leather chair and in the kitchen nook, where Grandma sewed and kept her stash of foil-wrapped Hostess Ding Dongs. I loved leafing through the stacks of *Jet* magazine, reading about the lives of famous and regular Black people. And I'll always remember the warm, inviting smells—Palmolive dish soap, Jergens lotion, frying bacon—that I identified with one thing: LOVE.

Because that home meant love to me, I was shocked to hear the story of how my grandparents came to live there—to learn that the process had been marred by hate. It was the mid-1940s, and my grandpa wanted to live in a particular part of town where there were new homes. However, he couldn't just call up a realtor and ask to see one.

Real estate agents and bankers made "gentlemen's agreements" with one another not to show or sell houses in certain areas to Black buyers. The homes were for white people only. So even if the laws didn't state that Black people couldn't live there, the practices of people in charge ensured that they wouldn't.

In some cases, these agreements actually were (and still are) in print, in what is known as "restrictive covenants"—bylaws of a new housing development or wording in a property title that explicitly excluded people based on race (and sometimes religion). In this way, northern cities created segregated environments while critiquing or looking down on southern states for their Jim Crow laws.

My grandparents' wedding day, 1941.
They moved to Empire Avenue the next day.

My grandpa was a proud (and stubborn) man. He had a vision and would not be deterred. He would go under the cover of night to look at the outsides of homes for sale. Then he found a white man to pose as a buyer. This man bought the house, deeded the property to my grandpa, and was willing to be paid back over time. He acted as buyer and bank so that my grandpa could live where he pleased, and in this way, they circumvented this racist practice being imposed on Black people.

My grandparents' new neighbors weren't too pleased to see who was actually moving in. No one brought casseroles to welcome *this* newlywed couple onto the block. Instead, they began to circulate a petition to force my grandparents' removal. Grandma said she got on her knees and prayed for God to protect her family and her home. After a while, the neighbors gave up on the petition, and my grandparents had their kids and went on living their lives. Grandpa lived in that house until his death in 1976. Grandma lived there for fifty years.

I experienced the tight-knit nature of Spokane's African American community (about 2 percent of the population) firsthand, at Bethel A.M.E. Church and with my grandparents' lifelong friends. Together, they had formed their own social clubs, baseball teams, newspapers, civic organizations, restaurants, and hangout places. They endured a total lack of representation in the professions (there were no Black dentists, doctors, or police officers, and only one or two teachers when my dad was growing up in the 1950s) and in government.

I recall how they spoke with pride about how one of their own, James Chase, who owned an auto shop (with Elmo Dalbert, another Black man), rose to become the city's first Black mayor in 1981. As young men, Mr. Chase and Mr. Dalbert had hopped a train from Texas with nothing but a desire for freedom and opportunity. My own ancestors migrated from North Carolina in the early 1900s, among the first African Americans to settle in Spokane. My grandparents were in the first generation born there.

I drew many elements of this story from my family's life in Spokane. My grandpa wanted to be a journalist but lost all his savings in 1930 when many banks failed; my great-grandma lived around the corner on Providence Avenue and always had ginger ale in her fridge; there were two Black minor league baseball players, Maury Wills and Tommy Davis, who sometimes threw around a ball with my dad (both men went on to play with the 1960s Los Angeles Dodgers championship team); and there was a prank involving a baseball glove

My Great Uncle Melburn's baseball team.

(my dad removed the strings to get back at his younger brother for something—no one can remember what). Like Melvin, my dad was set up for a school dance; he actually feigned sickness and got out of it. My dad also struggled with a stutter.

The North Pole was a soda fountain down the street where my dad and his siblings went; and a local TV variety show called *Starlit Stairway* featured kids and their talents. The Harlem Club was also a real place, and it was somewhat contro-versial. Owned by a Black man from the South, it was an establishment Black people enjoyed frequenting—but only two days of the week. The rest of the days were for white people only. The fact

1930s Harlem Club.

that a Black man maintained a segregated dining and dancing establishment points to the racism that was casually accepted by white people, who were the vast majority. They didn't want it any other way, so to be viable as a business, the owner kept it segregated. The Harlem Club burned down in 1951 (a few years before Melvin's story is set), and although the stated cause was faulty wiring, family sources tell me the true cause was never really known.

Of course, the historical event of Emmett Till's brutal murder at the hands of two white men is well documented, and for many Black Americans, seeing the picture of this boy's mutilated body in *Jet* magazine was a traumatic and defining moment. As this photo and others (such as one of his mother, Mamie Till-Mobley, grieving over his casket) circulated the globe, many became aware of the vicious hatred toward Black people in the South, and many rose up to say "no more" (very much like the worldwide protests that followed the murders of George Floyd and Breonna Taylor in 2020). One of those people was Rosa Parks, who eventually embarked on a speaking tour around the country to tell people about the need for civil rights in the South. She was not planning to visit Spokane after her stop in Seattle, but local NAACP officers entreated her to come, and she agreed. She spoke at Spokane's Calvary Baptist Church on March 30, 1956.

I don't know who introduced Mrs. Parks that night, but I like imagining it was a fourteen-year-old boy named Melvin Robinson, a boy who always had it within him to speak up.

A Note on the Use of the Word *Negro*:

Names are important. Some names are put on us, and others we choose for ourselves. While *Black* and *African American* are names we have chosen for ourselves as a community today, in Melvin's era, the term most Black people preferred was *Negro*. The word comes from the Spanish word *negro*, which means "black." It was what the Portuguese and Spanish called the African peoples they first encountered. Although to our ears it may sound strange or even offensive, from the eighteenth century through the late 1960s, *Negro* actually was considered the politest term and the one most Black people identified with.

The outspoken Black nationalist Marcus Garvey formed the Universal Negro Improvement Association in 1914 to mobilize African-descended people around the world to unite for their human rights. W. E. B. DuBois (civil rights activist and one of the founders of the NAACP) and Carter G. Woodson (called "the father of Black history" and the founder of Negro History Week—later Black History Month) used *Negro* in the titles of their nonfiction books. I used it throughout *Mighty Inside* to lend historical accuracy, and because in 1955 it was the preferred term of Black people, even though we no longer use it for ourselves today.

ACKNOWLEDGMENTS

I often hear authors say things like, "This story has been over ten years in the making," and I can now add myself to this group. In my case, it's been about twenty years since I started dreaming and pondering how to get this story down on the page. Many thanks to my editor, Arthur A. Levine, for believing in this story's potential, helping me find its center, and releasing it out into the world (while also providing insights about the Jewish experience and corrections to my clumsy use of Yiddish). Arthur, we found our way to the finish line, together, and I will always be grateful for your partnership, your advocacy, and your commitment to publishing stories from under-represented communities. Thank you to Meghan Maria McCullough for your behind-the-scenes assistance and careful reading of the manuscript, and to Anamika Bhatnagar for an incredibly thorough copyedit (your organizational skills and attention to detail are beyond measure!). Vaughn Fender, it is always exciting for authors to see visual artists work their magic to produce what will be a reader's first impression of our long-labored-over creations; thank you for taking time to understand Melvin and for designing a most fetching cover for his story. And to all the other great people at Levine Querido, including Antonio Gonzalez Cerna and Alex Hernandez, I look forward to working together to get Melvin's mighty fine voice out into the world.

To my marvelous and mighty agent, Regina Brooks: You have been such a champion for me and my work, believing when I wasn't sure. Thank you for always dreaming bigger.

Thank you to my dearest friends who have each played a role in helping me remain constant to this story, through companionship on writing getaways, check-ins that kept me anchored in the midst of societal and racial turmoil, and sharing the stresses of parenting in quarantine: Jenny Vaughn Hall, Denee White, Carla Saulter, Fina Arnold, Janet Chu, and Sara Easterly. Thank you to Rev. Dr. Brenda Salter-McNeil, whose words so many years ago that I was "pregnant with the possibility" of being a children's author reverberate to this day and keep me going with each and every project.

I'm grateful that in the midst of trying to birth this book, I was warmly received into a support group of committed professionals, affectionately known as the Mouse House. Thank you for being an encouraging circle of writers who celebrate each other's wins. Jolie Stekly, thank you for the "Writing and Mindset" class that provided fuel to keep going and connected me to even more passionate writers with whom to share this challenging journey.

Several people gave generously of their time to read this story in manuscript form and gave invaluable feedback in areas where I needed their perspective and personal insights. Yvette Fujimura Terada, thank you for your friendship and for entrusting me with your experiences as the daughter of Japanese Americans who were unjustly imprisoned in the World War II internment camps. Also, thank you for introducing me to the works of poet Suma Yagi and activist/healer/documentary producer Satsuki Ina, which were critical to my understanding of the generational impacts of that horrendous injustice. I especially commend Ina's work *Children of the Camps* to anyone looking to understand better; its message will remain relevant as long as xenophobia exists and people maintain an insider/outsider mentality.

I don't know when or how the reality that Melvin would be a kid who stuttered came into the picture, but I want to first thank my dad for sharing with me about his own experience, and also Austin

Burnett, a high school student with a passion to reach other kids who stutter with his own writing and illustrating. When I met Austin and he pulled out his book-in-progress, it was in the exact same brand and color notebook as the one I was using for Melvin, which we took as a sign that we were meant to meet and were on the right track with our respective projects. It was, as Lenny would say, beshert.

An enormous thank you to Jerome Ellis, whom I first heard on *This American Life* in an incredible story about confronting disfluency discrimination, for being willing to read the manuscript and for his enthusiastic response. His and others' reflections on what it means to speak with a stutter opened my eyes to the perspective that a stutter is not something to fix, but offers an opportunity to experience a different kind of relationship to time. Those who stutter challenge the Western fixation on efficiency, productivity, and fluid speech, and can release us from our need for predictability and control. The book *Stuttering* by Marty Jezer was also instrumental in helping me understand the stuttering experience.

My desire was to create an homage to all of the fiercely proud African Americans who made their mark on Spokane and the Northwest region, including my ancestors. An incredible resource on African Americans in the Northwest is Dr. Quintard Taylor, whose books and website (www.blackpast.org) were a great help in my research. Jerrelene Williamson's *African Americans in Spokane* was an invaluable resource, as well. I'm deeply grateful to Ms. Williamson's efforts to keep the stories of our people in this area alive. Thank you to Gwenn Smith Olson for all the genealogy and record-keeping you've done on our joint family. To extended cousins Butch Freeman and George Freeman, and to Spokane friend Dr. Mona Lake Jones, thank you for the wonderful times of storytelling you offered.

My most personal and deepest-felt thanks are reserved for my dad, mom, Aunt Kathy, and Uncles Steve and Neil, who were willing to gather in Spokane one weekend several years ago at the home of longtime family friend Joan Butler to tell me their memories of growing up. I'll always cherish that time and the laughter we shared. Thank you, Uncle Steve, for preserving and cataloging the old family photos and being the repository of family names and connections. Thank you all for being the village to my generation when we were growing up—and now for the next generation, as well. You supported me with everything I needed as I struggled to find my way to this finished story (including its title—thank you, Aunt Kathy!). I hope it makes you proud. To my grandparents, William and Willa Tucker, your dedication to our family and to fighting in your own way for the right to live how and where you wanted left a legacy for which your offspring are eternally grateful. Of course, I never met the man who bought the house for my grandparents, but finding his name, his spouse's name, and that of my grandpa on a deed was a thrill: Armond and Bessie Caro were allies for my family in 1941.

Thank you to my biggest ally, Matt, for your steadfast support—we will be riding the ups and downs together until the end. And finally, forever love to my daughters, Skye and Umbria, who through surreptitious notes and verbal reminders, continue to insist that I write.

Some Notes on This Book's Production

The art for the jacket was created by Vaughn Fender using hand-drawn elements and digitized textures. Melvin's portrait was digitally drawn and edited. The title was hand-drawn and vectorized using Adobe Illustrator.

The body text was set in Freight Text, a serif typeface known for its clean legibility, designed by Joshua Darden and published by GarageFonts in 2005. The display, set in Alright Sans and designed by Jackson Cavanaugh for Okay Type in 2009, is characterized by simple details and a warm underlying structure. MVB Emmascript, originally drawn by Kanna Aoki in 1996 and adapted into a font by Mark van Bronkhorst, is utilized within the Author's Note to add life to the photo captions.

The text was set by Westchester Publishing Services in Danbury, CT.

The book was printed on 98 GSM Yunshidai Ivory uncoated woodfree FSC™-certified paper and bound in China.

Production was supervised by
Leslie Cohen and Freesia Blizard

Book design by
Vaughn Fender

Edited by
Arthur A. Levine

LEVINE QUERIDO